"Not just entertaining, but timely, as well. The public as a whole seems eager to declare the war on terror over. As this book makes crystal clear, we may have seen only the beginning. Well researched and provocative."

--Charles Faddis, Retired CIA operative
who led the first team of agents into
Iraq after 9/11 & author of *Operation
Aphrodite*

"Chadwell hits a bulls-eye with the topical theme of maritime piracy. The novel is interesting, exciting and riveting throughout. As a law enforcement executive with experience in the arena of homeland security, I was impressed with Chadwell's accurate depiction of the realities of maritime piracy. This is a must read for those who enjoy and action-packed novel grounded in a current and a very real issue. This novel rivals many of Tom Clancy's best sellers!"

--Carlos Rojas, Deputy Chief of Police
& former head of Homeland Security for the
City of Santa Ana, Calif.

"If you are looking for a book from a sensationalist author with no real life experience then look elsewhere, but if you enjoy getting information from the sourc, then read this book. The author is an experienced journalist with over 20 years of naval experience and it shows!" --John Konrad, author of *Fire on the
Horizon* and editor of gCaptain.com

"This book opens like a Tom Clancy novel...interesting geographical, social and historical background as a way of setting the scene for the action to follow. Like Clancy, Chadwell's topic is relevant to current events, and serves as a cautionary tale for the threats faced by the West today. I hope this becomes required reading for U.S. Navy SEALs and the Royal Navy Special Boat Service."

--Steven Chesser, Retired Naval Officer,
U.S. Navy

Hunt of the Sea Wolves is a work of fiction. Names, characters, places, and incidents either are the product of the author's imagination or are used fictitiously. Any resemblance to actual persons, living or dead, events, or locales is entirely coincidental.

Cover illustration: Duncan Long

For

U.S. Forces

Thanks you for fighting the good fight.

Follow *Hunt of the Sea Wolves* blog, www.huntoftheseawolves.net/blog

& on Facebook

Death is coming from the sea.

HUNT of the
SEA WOLVES

JOHN CHADWELL

Greek astronomer, mathematician, and geographer, Claudius Ptolemaeus (87 – 150 AD),

made one of the earliest references to the Andaman and Nicobar Islands, which were inhabited for centuries primarily by the Great Andamanese, who collectively represented the various tribes: Jarawa, Jangil, Onge, and the Sentinelese. The island chain first fell under European rule when the Danish East India Company arrived in the 1750s.

For more than three centuries, pirates have plied the waters around these islands mainly because of their proximity to the northern entrance of the Strait of Malacca, the main trade route to the Far East.

Today was no different, but this time the pirates were in a fight for their lives as a pitched battle raged aboard the small inter-island freighter. The ship drifted dead in the water within sight of a small island, one of the five hundred seventy-two-islands in the Andaman and Nicobar archipelago, a territory of India.

The rusting freighter was on fire from stem to stern. A ragged-looking gang of thirty Asian marauders fought determinedly against the eighteen Indian Marine Commando Force, or MARCOS, operators. The pirates, armed with ancient weapons, ranging from shotguns to a Thompson submachine gun, left behind by some nameless American soldier in an equally nameless conflict somewhere in Southeast Asia, to an assortment of machetes and spears, were being forced across the burning decks toward the bow.

As the operators who were already aboard the ship pushed relentlessly forward, others fast- roped down to the deck from a hovering Sea King Mk 42C helicopter. The pirate with the shotgun fired up at one of the operators as he slid down the heavy rope, holding on with one hand and his legs, and firing his Sterling MP-4 sub-machine gun.

The heavy shotgun slugs hit the operator below his armored vest, cutting him in half. His upper torso hit the deck, while his legs fell into the sea. His last fleeting thought was to kill the man who killed him. However, his strength quickly waned and his vision dimmed as his blood flowed across a cargo hold hatch.

The weapon slipped from his fingers as another operator hit the deck and pulled his dying comrade's body behind a winch motor. With one last look and a squeeze on the dying man's shoulder, the operator eased his friend into death.

He stood and steadied himself against a cargo boom mast. In a single effortless motion, he slipped off a sleek, high-tech carbon compound bow, pulled an aluminum arrow with a razor-edged, cyanide-tipped head, and sent it streaking across the ship into the chest of the man who had killed his friend.

The pirate with the Thompson fired up at the helicopter. Three holes stitched the side just below the pilot. He jerked the controls, causing the chopper to bank sharply and disappeared into the night sky.

At six feet two, Captain Anumita Roy Vajpayee led a corporal and a sergeant through the flames, as he fired his MP-5 sub-machine gun, killing two of the pirates as he sprinted up the starboard ladder to the next deck. They spread out inside the starboard passageway. The corporal kicked in a wooden door, stepped into the mess decks, and was nearly decapitated as a crazed-looking Chinese pirate swung a rusted saber at him. The young operator froze, just as Captain Vajpayee shoved him aside and shot the man twice through the heart and once between the eyes. The old pirate dropped at the corporal's feet.

Sergeant Bhupad Ali stepped into the room behind Captain Vajpayee. At the opposite end of the room, two more pirates stood over a huddled group of the ship's terrified crew, who were sprawled face down on the deck. Before the two operators could react, one of the pirates calmly shot the man at his feet in the back. The other pirate touched the muzzle of his weapon against a boy's neck. His finger started to squeeze the trigger then his hand jerked spasmodically and the rifle clattered to the floor as a hollow-point bullet ripped into his face.

For the fraction of a second that he had left to live, the other pirate did not comprehend why his friend was on his back staring up at him without a face. Then he turned and glanced at a porthole to his right. He saw the neat, round bullet hole. He squinted focusing on the small hole, then as his eyes opened wider and refocused, he saw the sniper outside standing on a small helo-landing platform on the stern of the ship. The pirate knew he was a dead man before the sniper took his second shot. He started to cry out to the God who he had cursed his entire life as the heavy round shattered the porthole and then struck him in the mouth. The sniper, Corporal Abdul-Baari Singh, chambered another round with satisfaction.

Not inclined to taking prisoners, the operators had dispatched all of the pirates before the sun's first rays appeared over the horizon. As the last marine operative stepped aboard the hovering helo, a small boat out of the capital city of Port Blair heaved to and fro in the swells just beyond the cordon of police patrol boats.

One of the scuba divers vacationing from Australia struggled to keep his footing while aiming his Sony camcorder, capturing the Sea King as it departed from the smoldering hulk.

In a world of instant linkups and wireless networks, it was only a matter of racing back to Port Blair and the Sainik Vishram Ghar hotel, where he could call the local BBC News outlet and stream the video to them in New Delhi.

Within an hour after receiving the amateur footage, the BBC affiliate was airing it throughout the Asia Pacific, Australasia, and South Asia Middle East. A BBC newsman's voice over declared, "Indian anti-terrorist Special Forces were able to thwart the efforts of a reputed

Aceh rebel cell that has been terrorizing shipping lanes in the area, stealing entire cargos, killing the crews, and setting the ships adrift."

The dizzying footage was replaced by the image of a stately British official, identified as Sir Thomas Burkenshire, whose sound bite forewarned, "Modern piracy as a terrorist weapon has been neglected far too long and it will come back to haunt every civilized nation."

The term *Moro* was coined by Spanish colonizers in the Philippines and applied to Filipino Muslims who lived mostly in the southern islands of Mindanao, Palawan, and the Sulu Archipelago. The Moros have carried on an almost non-stop guerrilla campaign against all non-Muslim in the Philippines, whether they were fellow Filipinos, invading Conquistadors in 1521, or the American army in the early twentieth century. For the past 500 years, the Muslims of the Sulu Archipelago and southwestern Mindanao have fought against foreign rulers and no central Philippine government has been able to wrest complete control over Moro controlled territories.

Toward the end of their 300-year reign in the Philippines, the Spaniards encouraged and supported privateers to attack from the sea in order to break down Moro resistance. On December 21, 1751, Spain's Governor-General of Manila signed a decree that gave the privateers' free reign to exterminate the Moslems of Mindanao and Sulu with "fire and sword and no quarter for Moros of any age or either sex." Visayan corsairs were fitted out with the authority to destroy the Moros at sea. All crops would be destroyed and the land would be desolated. Moreover, if not killed outright, every Moro would be enslaved.

At the outset of the decree, a Royal fifth of all spoils went to the Spanish throne, but this policy was later abolished to permit the privateers to retain all the plunder, as well as to encourage them to exact maximum cruelty on the Moros.

Privateer fleets sailed out of Manila to do battle against the Moros in southern seas. Fearless and fanatical, the Moros defeated the privateers at every turn. They soon gained control of the seas and united in a jihad against Spain.

Handily defeating Spain, the Moros were not content to live peacefully with their neighbors, be they fellow Filipinos or the ancestors of foreigners who had settled in the islands. In 1775, a fleet of twenty Moro vessels with 4,000 warriors set sail to attack the British, who had forcefully taken Manila from the Spanish in 1762. All but six British soldiers were killed during a two-pronged attack on the fort from the sea and the jungle.

Fueled by the success of their campaign against the British, the Moro leader set his sights again on the remaining Spanish at Zamboanga. Though the Spaniards were able to repel the Moros in this battle, their days were numbered in the Philippines.

The Moros fortified the town of Mambarao on Mindaro Island to provide a haven to their pirate fleets. However, the fortification proved impossible to defend and a Royal Spanish squadron drove the Moros out of Mambarao.

Long years of warfare while trying to drive out the military forces of Spain, France, and America, were interrupted by meager periods of tentative peace. Little was accomplished in curbing the Moro appetite for warfare until the arrival of Captain John J. "Black Jack" Pershing, who had his own version of fanatical terrorist to deal with in the form of the juramentados.

The term, which means *oath*, was first applied to the Moro guerrillas in 1876. The practice of "running juramentado" was a religious rite involving the waging of a jihad upon infidels, in the same vein as today's suicide car bombers. At first, the juramentados were bands of determined fighters who willingly sacrificed their lives in order to kill Christians. Individuals would run through the streets—for the lack of a handy Toyota pickup or Mercedes sedan—to kill as many unbelievers as possible before being gunned down themselves. Enjoined in the Qur'an, the jihad against unbelievers in its pure form was considered a bona-fide organized warfare against Christians. Juramentado was the degenerate form of jihad evolved by the Sulu Moros.

Those sworn to juramentado of Mindanao and Sulu were treacherous killers. Of all the Mohammedans worldwide, only the Moros practiced the ritual of juramentado. For the committed individual to sacrificing himself was not considered suicide, but rather a positive self-destruction. Rather than risking eternal hell, "juramentado" assured for them great fame in the next life as one who had killed many Christians.

Then as now, there were certain rituals that needed to be done before setting out on a mission. The juramentados were mainly young, impressionable boys. They would undergo elaborate preparations of the body before the running of juramentado so that God would look on them favorably when they appeared before him. First, they gathered to hear the Imams, or priests, who inflamed the youths to seek out martyrdom. After a solemn farewell to their parents to obtain their "permission," the young men would band together and set out to wage holy war.

An elaborate grooming process finalized with shaving their eyebrows and cutting their hair short. They tightly bound themselves, including their genitals, so they could remain on their feet as long as possible after being wounded by blade or bullet. Over the bindings, they donned white robes, called the *jubba*. They topped off the suicidal regalia with a white turban and a charm, an *anting-anting*, at their waist to protect them from the enemy's weapons.

They paid just as much attention to cleaning and polishing their bladed weapons, the kris and barong. It apparently did not occur to them to strap explosives to their chests. Finally, ready to conduct their holy war, the juramentado would search out as many Christians gathered in one place as possible. As he shouted, "There is no God but Allah," the juramentado would charge into the crowd swinging his weapons, decapitating and disemboweling as many Christians as possible, no matter if they were adults, children, male, female, military, or civilian (the same rules of engagement that the Spanish gave the privateers for hunting down the Moros). The only thing that drove them was killing as many Christians as possible before becoming a martyr in death. Juramentado martyrs entered paradise astride a magnificent white horse, and each Christian dispatched became a slave.

Nearly unstoppable, even when pumped full of bullets, the fanatical juramentado Moros of Sulu and Mindanao were some of the most deadly combatants in history. They were so fierce and so deadly that the weapon of choice for the U.S. Army in the Philippines was the Colt .45. It was the only handgun that could knock a crazed juramentado off his feet. Needless to say, few juramentados were taken alive.

History has a way of repeating itself. On the other hand, perhaps the jihad is just so engrained in the minds of radical Muslims that to this day they still recognize the strategic advantage of emulating the juramentados, who were the original terrorists, as they begin to collaborate with or take over pirate activities.

By 1908, piracy in the Sulu had exploded. Today, American forces continue to assume that piracy is a thing of the distant past. It was a mistake in the early twentieth century and it is a mistake today to believe that the ever-resourceful Moros would pass up an opportunity to exploit America's lack of historical insight and appreciation of the Moros' perspective, which was that piracy remains a legitimate source of income to fund their cause.

In a hauntingly predictive note that could have been penned today to explain the mindset of the modern jihadist, Governor-General Pershing may have stated it best when he wrote on February 28, 1913, "The nature of the Moro is such that he is not at all overawed or impressed by an overwhelming force. If he takes a notion to fight, it is regardless of the number of men he thinks are to be brought against him. You cannot bluff him. There are already enough troops on the island of Jolo to smother the defiant element, but the conditions are such that if we attempt such a thing, the loss of life among innocent women and children would be very great. It is estimated that there are only about 300 arms altogether on the island of Jolo and that these are assembled on the top of Mount Bagsak in fortified cottas [forts]. This situation, as I stated at the beginning, is a difficult one. I fully appreciate your confidence in my ability to handle the situation and you may rest assured that my best efforts are being put forth to carry out the purpose of our undertaking—disarmament with as little disturbance and as little loss of life as possible."

From the American perspective, Pershing successfully halted the Moro "insurrection." The Moros, however, looked at the struggles against American forces as courageous "last stand" battles, much like Americans look at the defenders of the Alamo as a heroic fight for independence. Present day Moros consider the battles as important links in the Filipino struggle for nationhood.

Over the next few decades, the Moros' resolve was fortified with the rise of Islamic nationalism. Muslim separatists established the Moro Islamic Liberation Front (MILF) in 1984. Their goal was to acquire independence and autonomy for the Muslim regions. They immediately set out to establish an independent Islamic state in the southern Philippines.

Most of the MILF is made up of Filipino Maguinanaon and Iranun ethnic groups with an estimated strength of up to 120,000 fighters. The principal terrorist network, called the Abu Sayyaf, or *Bearer of the Sword*, has taken up the banner of juramentados in advancing their goals through any means, including kidnapping for ransom, murder on land and at sea, and suicidal missions to rid not only the Sulu, but the world of infidels.

The Sulu Sea is situated between Borneo, Palawan, and the Philippines. Politically, the Sulu province consists of over 400 scattered and almost isolated islands, extending from Zamboanga southwestward towards Borneo. The islands within the Sulu Sea make up the Sulu archipelago, the southernmost part of the Philippines, and divide the Sulu and the Celebes seas.

3

Therefore, it was that on a November night, under a full moon, the converted freighter

Eastern Explorer was making its way through these still treacherous waters. Every day, foreign-flagged freighters and tankers of every description and tonnage, as well as thousands of fishing vessels, ranging from commercial purse-seiners to traditional fishing boats handmade from Palomaria trees, transited the sea lanes past the islands of Jolo, Pangutaran, Samales, Siasi, Sibuto, and Tawi-Tawi.

The Eastern Explorer was a ship that had gone through many transformations in her more than sixty years of service. She was commissioned in 1944, as the Molly Pitcher. She replaced another exactly like her, the West Portal. A German U-boat sank the West Portal in the South Atlantic, after she had played a crucial role as one of many cargo transports that were part of the Western Task Force (WTF). WTF had delivered Maj. Gen. George S. Patton, Jr., the tanks of the Second Armored Division and Seventieth Tank Battalion, and over thirty-four thousand troops that landed at Safi, as they mounted the attack on Casablanca.

Having survived more than one torpedo run at her, Molly Pitcher went through her first transformation at war's end as she was sold then converted to an island steamer named the Atlantic Sun and used primarily to ferry pilgrims to the new Jewish state.

In 1951, she was recruited back into government service as a troop ship to transport British soldiers, still war weary from the years of fighting throughout Europe, to Korea. Having served valiantly as a floating home for thousands of men who just wanted to return to England alive and in one piece, she was ingloriously decommissioned after the 1953 armistice. She was then shuttled off to one the of many mothball fleets scattered around the world.

Rusting and forgotten, she was just days away from being ripped apart for scrap when she received a reprieve from a faceless, nameless British bureaucrat who came looking for a vessel of an indeterminate heritage that would go unnoticed as she plied the waterways of the world while undertaking a particularly mysterious and unpleasant task.

Outfitted with sophisticated communications and navigational equipment, along with a fresh coat of paint, and her new name, the Eastern Explorer steamed stealthily on a sea that, apart from her presence, appeared utterly empty. Her bow cut through the black, phosphorescent water. In the distance, lights from Zamboanga City on Mindanao flickered on the horizon.

As a British ensign snapped in the wind high above the main deck from the radio mast just above the bridge, Rudy Carbullido stood as the lone sentry at the ship's bow. A Guamanian of Chamorro ancestry—Indonesian with a healthy mix of Spanish, Filipino, and other Micronesian strains—Rudy had signed on as a crewman two months earlier when the ship made a stopover at his home island.

Those aboard the ship were well aware of the Sulu Archipelago's piratical reputation. They were concerned enough to post an armed seaman both fore and aft, but apparently not concerned enough to train the men how to use the automatic weapons they carried.

Each man also carried a single ammo clip, but he was not allowed to put it in the weapon, lest he accidentally shoot one of his shipmates. This was not as absurd as it might sound. All aboard, excepting for the officers, were recruited from the least skilled laborers as they hung out at docks around the world desperately looking for employment aboard any departing vessel.

The crew might have also been better served, or at least more vigilant while acting as lookouts as they transited the dangerous waterways through the Philippines, if the officers had reminded them that Mindanao was the stronghold for the Abu Sayyaf. Therefore, the crew had little thought of the political complexities taking place just over the horizon. If they had, perhaps they would have been better prepared to defend the old ship and themselves.

Despite the fact that Zamboanga City was command central for the Mindanao Island Invasion Strike Force, whose mission it was to eradicate the guerrilla organization, Abu Sayyaf continued to strike out against the Philippine government through bombings, extortion, hijackings, kidnapping and ransoming Westerners, and assassinations, in its quest to establish a separate Islamic state

Rudy took a drag on the non-filtered cigarette, careful to cup the glowing embers in the palm of his hand so those on the bridge would not see that he was smoking while on watch. Moments later, he took a long, leisurely last drag, and then ground the butt against the heel of his shoe before tossing it over the side. He looked out at the flawless sea. Its beauty and awesomeness never ceased to humble him, even after all the years he had spent aboard the ship.

4

As a citizen of Guam, a territory of the United States, Guamanian men were eligible to enlist into the U.S. military. Most chose the navy because of the presence of Naval Base Guam, which, in one form or another, had been the major employer, as well as protector, ever since the

American forces retook the island from the Japanese three years after they overran it in 1941. Four years after the war ended in the Pacific, President Truman signed the Organic Act, converting Guam into an unincorporated territory of the United States, which gave it limited self-governing authority.

The navy and other U.S. military branches were the main employers until the Japanese invaded the island once again—this time as tourists. A building boom began and new hotels sprang up around the island. But when the economy in Japan slipped, fewer tourists visited Guam. This, along with the fact that beginning with President Clinton's administration, many military installations were closed or reorganized, the unemployment rate climbed to over seventeen percent. So many of Guam's brightest and best continued to join the military and leave their Pacific paradise.

Rudy enlisted right out of high school in 1965. Within the week, he was bound for San Diego, where he was immersed in an alien world called boot camp. He was suddenly surrounded by several thousand frightened teenagers who were mainly there because they did not want to be drafted into the army only to end up in the rice paddies of Vietnam.

During the next twelve weeks, Rudy was transformed. He slowly evolved from a carefree island boy who wanted nothing more than to serve his adopted country to a disillusioned, resentful minority within minorities. He realized very early on in the process that the white senior enlisted instructors, particularly those who had served in the South Pacific, considered him no better than a *Filipino*. As a Guamanian, he could not tolerate this.

While a degree of equality was being parceled out to women, blacks, and gays during the seventies, the U.S. Navy continued to relegate Filipinos to a position of servitude, they could only work on the mess decks where they waited on other enlisted sailors, or in the wardrooms, where they served the whims of the ships' officers.

Only after they had advanced to the rank of seaman and had to choose a rating, or job specialty such as electronics or engineering, to "strike" for enlisted rank of third class petty officer, were they able to choose an alternative career path for themselves. However, since advancement was still a slow process that had not changed appreciatively since World War II, most of the Filipinos were middle aged, by that time. So most elected to stay where they where were comfortable and spent their entire careers as Mess Management Specialists, as the navy liked to call them, rather than what everyone else knew them as, mess cooks.

From the very first day in boot camp, Rudy began his twenty-year campaign to get it across to anyone within earshot that he was Guamanian, not Filipino, and that he would never be content to be a mess cook. During the battery of tests, he scored high on recognition of Morse Code, which qualified him for radio school. Since the war was picking up-tempo in Viet Nam, the navy, in one of its rare instances of common sense, Rudy thought, felt it would be better served with a radioman than another mess cook.

In one of life's ironies, after six months of intense training in Morse Code, typing, and radio message handling, Rudy was sent to his first duty station, a communications ship, where, because he was the junior man in the department, he was immediately shunted off to the mess decks to serve as a mess cook for six months.

During this time, his bitterness and racial intolerance were fine-tuned by having to work alongside the young Filipinos he had fought to separate himself from, along with other minorities who had been "volunteered" by their chief petty officers.

By the time Rudy finally made it into the radio compartments, he had long forgotten most of the Morse Code, which didn't matter, anyway because the navy was by then using teletype machines and he never heard code again.

Over the next two decades, outwardly, Rudy was the ultimate professional, advancing to the rank of chief petty officer. But beneath the surface, he never forgot or forgave the years of personal slights and racial jabs to the ribs he received from his so-called shipmates.

On a hot July afternoon in 1989, Rudy packed his seabag for the last time, tucked his discharge papers into his Naugahyde briefcase, and walked down the aft gangway of his last ship that had pulled into Guam to let him off before continuing on to Yokosuka.

After reporting in to the transit barracks, because he was a short-timer he was only required to call in each day, which he did from his cousin's home, until he found a small place of his own. A week later, he had his separation papers and a navy pension of twelve hundred fifty dollars that was electronically deposited each month into his checking account.

It took him one more day to figure out that no one had changed in his small town. No one, that is, except for him. He had underestimated the worldliness he had acquired while in the navy. With his navy pension, he was well off by Guamanian standards. He didn't have to work unless he wanted to, but there were few decent paying jobs to be had on the island and he sensed the immediate resentment of those around him when he applied for one of the few openings at the Naval Station—in the mess hall.

When an Australian merchant ship pulled in the harbor one day, Rudy made it a point to bump into one of the officers on shore leave that night. When he told the officer he had served as a radioman in the U.S. Navy for twenty years, the Australian asked how fast Rudy was at Morse Code. Another irony of the changing times: while the navy no longer used the code, merchant ships still required radio operators to be code-qualified and proficient on the speed key, which Rudy had never used.

The officer said the ship was short handed on the deck crew and as a veteran with years of experience at sea, it shouldn't be a problem for Rudy to get his merchant seaman papers if he wanted the job.

So began Rudy's second career at sea. He said goodbye to his cousin and sailed on the Monday morning tide. Today, he couldn't recall how many different ships he had served aboard, of all flags and with all nationalities. Most of his crewmates were uneducated and desperate. He told no one of his naval service or pension, content to work the long hours for months at a time.

It wasn't unusual for him to leave one ship in Singapore, sign on another bound for Amsterdam, and then shift over to a third carrying a cargo through Panama and up to Los Angeles. Every so often, he had a yen to go home for a visit and he would catch a ship headed for Bangkok, Taiwan, or Manila, with a stopover in Guam.

5

This was his third round trip aboard the Eastern Explorer. He looked out across the moon lit sea that was flawlessly smooth except for the wake the ship sliced through the black water. Occasionally, a flying fish would erupt from the wake, slap its tail, and propel itself effortlessly as it glided on silvery wings away from the ship. He thought of their last port call in Australia, and the Indonesian girl he met on the beach. Though they were complete opposites when it came to culture, religion, and age, they were both far from home and lonely.

He smiled at the thought of her young, dark body. They had spent three glorious days together and had parted with no misconceptions about ever contacting one another again. He would remember her fondly, though he believed she was a prostitute on holiday. That would explain her nimbleness and unconcern at bedding down with a Christian.

He turned back from daydreaming and looked back at the ship that had been home for the past three years. He had crewed on worse ships. The chow was okay, and unlike other crewmen, he didn't mind the long hours on watch. Most of the officers kept to themselves, and those who, by the nature of their duties, mingled with the deck hands, treated him well enough because of his experience.

As he looked up at the lighted bridge, he wondered once again why the ship's owners had spent as much as they did refitting a ship as old as the Eastern Explorer. His many years at sea, particularly those in the navy, gave him a unique understanding among his deck force peers of the worth a ship held to its owners.

In October, the day before the ship left its European homeport on its regularly scheduled deployment to Japan, while most of the crew had gone ashore, he had decided to stay onboard. After finishing off James Michener's, *The Source*, for the second time, he had meandered through the ship, not looking for anything particular. He had never ventured, nor been permitted to do so, on to the bridge. Since no one was around, he decided to explore the forbidden spaces.

What he discovered on the bridge and in the adjacent radio space convinced him there was more to the Eastern Explorer than he had ever have imagined. As a chief radioman aboard the USS Estes, an amphibious force flagship that had served as the communications center for combat operations in-country Vietnam, he had worked with sophisticated communications gear, including crypto, which was located in obscure spaces deep in the ship where only those with the proper security clearances were permitted to enter.

He never said anything about his discovery, but from that point on, he was keenly interested in the goings and comings of the ship's officers, as well as the mysterious cargos that were loaded into one of the ship's three holds after normal working hours by men who he knew were not union stevedores.

One more thing set the Eastern Explorer apart from any other merchant he had crewed before. This was the first vessel that required the lookouts to carry automatic weapons while on watch.

He had heard of pirates hijacking ships and killing or setting adrift the crews, so he thought it a good idea that the lookouts were armed. But this presented yet another irony. Since he had served his time in the navy and not the marines or army, he had never used an automatic weapon, and had only spent a single day in boot camp on a firing range with the already obsolete M1 carbine. He wished the officers had at least taken the initiative to show him how to use the heavy weapon he carried slung across his chest.

Rudy wasn't a completely inexperienced when it came to firearms. He had fired a Remington single shot .22 rifle when he was a kid, but this hunk of scrap iron that weighed him down was an old World War II-era .30 caliber, M1918A2, Browning Automatic Rifle, or BAR. He wasn't even sure he knew how to slip the clip in it, should there be a need to do so. Moreover, the fact that he was sixty years old and stood only five feet tall didn't help when it came to lugging around the heavy weapon. He was thankful, though, that the officer had not insisted on adding the bipod and bandoleer, which would have topped out the weapon's weight at forty pounds.

From his experience, officers always lied to the crew, so he didn't believe the man who told him there was really no need for him to know how to load the BAR because there was little likelihood any pirates would attempt to go up against a ship as large and as fast as the Eastern Explorer. Besides, Rudy rationalized, the single clip he was permitted to carry wouldn't do much good against a band of thugs armed with the latest weapons terrorist dollars could buy.

He had enough time at sea to know better than to complain. There were too many men in too many ports who would gladly take over his job. This was because no matter how unpleasant the conditions might be, or how grueling the work, life aboard a merchant ship was eons removed from the dismal existence most of them led back home.

Therefore, he tended to his duties without complaint and filled his free hours, such as they were with reading every book he could get his hands on. He could read English, Spanish, Japanese, and some Mandarin, so whenever the ship pulled into any port in the Far East, the first stop he made ashore was at the booksellers, who paid scant attention to copyright laws. He could pick up the latest best seller, the ink virtually still wet, for as little as twenty-five cents.

He had made up his mind that this would be his last deployment. It was time to go home for good. Over the years, he had invested in his cousin's small tour business in Merizo, and he had recently wired funds to his cousin in order to buy another Ford van for the growing business.

Besides the money, he had signed on with the Eastern Explorer mainly because of its regular stops in Japanese ports. This gave him many opportunities to practice his conversational Japanese skills and to visit travel agencies in order to drop off his new brochures.

Japanese made up more than ninety percent of the tourists who came to Guam. Rudy figured these repeat visits to agencies, as well as the time he spent honing his Japanese skills, and learning the culture, would be worth their weight in gold when he returned home to join his cousin in running the business.

He lit another cigarette, his eighth during the four-hour watch. Again, he was diligent in cupping the flame in his hands. Because the ship was running dark in an attempt to navigate through the thousands of islands undetected, something as small as a lit match or glowing cigarette ember would stand out like a flare shot into the night sky.

But the ploy wasn't working. As the crew of the Eastern Explorer guided the big ship through a narrow passage between two islands, three small speedboats sped out from a hidden inlet.

Aboard the black boats, fifteen heavily armed Filipinos, all members of the Moro Islamic Liberation Front, the MILF, the extremist guerrilla organization, watched intently as they sped toward the big ship. Despite the fact it was running without lights, its position was given away, its dark form silhouetted against the coastal lights from Mindanao. In one of the three small boats, a man signaled with a red-filtered flashlight to those in the other boats.

The Eastern Explorer's bridge was bathed in the amber glow from the red "standing" lights. These were used not only to improve the bridge crew's night vision, but also to avoid detection—since red light rays don't travel as far as white light—on the occasion that someone stepped out on to the bridge wing and exposed the ship's interior to the outside.

As the rest of the crew stood at their duty stations, the navigation officer bent over the chart table plotting a change in course, which was a constant task when threading through the narrow sea-lanes of the Philippines.

"Captain, recommend we come right to zero one five degrees at 1945 hours," he said in a soft Yorkshire accent without looking up from the chart. He drew a line between islands. "Estimate remaining on that course for five minutes."

Captain Timothy Blackwell, a tall and angular man whose bearing and physical conditioning belied his age and proximity to enforced retirement from the British Merchant Navy, still took the position of command at sea as a badge of honor and loyalty. He was what some would call 'the common seaman's captain,' in that he would never ask a crewman to do something he had not done himself as he advanced through the ranks over the last thirty-five years. After his wife and two daughters, his loyalty was to his crew, first, then to his employer.

But Captain Blackwell, as one who had first gone to sea as a merchant seaman serving as a wiper aboard oil tanker Balder London, knew first hand a seaman's lot. He wasn't soft on his crews by any measure, but no man who served under him would claim he wasn't a just man.

He looked up at the clock as the time changed to 19:45. "Helmsman, come right to new course zero one five degrees," he said as he gazed out the window, noticing the full moon seemingly hovering just above the black water.

"Coming right to new course, zero one five degrees," the helmsman responded as he turned the wheel slightly and watched the compass swing to the new heading. "Now steering zero one five degrees, sir."

The captain peered through his binoculars across the bow. "Very well."

At the sound of clinking dishes, Blackwell turned to see Carlos Bagsic, the ship's Filipino steward, as he stepped onto the bridge with a steaming mug of coffee. He brought it over to the captain. "Coffee, Captain?" he said, handing the mug to Blackwell.

"Thank you, Carlos. That would hit the spot," Blackwell said. He took the mug gratefully, took a sip, eased back into his leather chair, and held the mug in both hands to warm them. He did not notice Carlos leave the bridge, nor the man's quick glance at each of the bridge crew.

Blackwell was distracted at the thought of home and a long-delayed fishing trip to Iceland with his son, Thomas. They had made up recently after two years of estrangement over Thomas' announcement that he was dropping out of university to explore the Middle East with a girl he had met in Tel Aviv, while backpacking during summer break.

It didn't bother Blackwell all that much that the girl was Jewish, but she did have a disturbing effect on Thomas, which Blackwell both admired and dreaded. If it were only a summer romance, he thought, but the girl seemed determined to recruit Thomas to her cause. Which cause that might be was still to be determined. But the boy had his hands full with her and Blackwell feared for his son's safety every time he went to Israel to see her.

7

The speedboats approached the Eastern Explorer from either side of the fantail. The noise from the ship's generators and compressors, as well as the cauldron churned up behind by the ship's prop, drowned out the sound from the boats' outboard motors. The ship towered over the three speedboats. One man in each boat wore night-vision goggles and scanned the fantail with his weapon for any sentries. They saw no one. Another man in each boat swung long ropes with grapnel hooks attached and heaved them up and over the ship's railings where they scraped noisily across the metal deck. Had there been an alert sentry, the guerrillas could have been stopped at this point.

The guerrillas pulled the ropes until they felt the grapnels snag something on deck. Once they felt the lines tighten, they paid no attention to the water that raced between the speedboats and the huge ship like a swirling river. They swung away from the boats and began to climb up toward the Eastern Explorer's main deck. After the men were aboard, they tossed the grapnel hooks overboard and the two boats pulled away and kept pace with the ship.

A door swung out from the superstructure carelessly and banged loudly against the bulkhead as a heavyset seaman in sweat-stained dungarees stepped out. He was nearing the end of his watch in the engine room and was in desperate need of a smoke, some chow, a hot shower, and then rack time. He stretched and yawned sleepily, scratched, and then glanced out to sea.

At first, the seaman was puzzled at what he saw. Just before dawn, the light could play tricks on you at sea. Was it a whale or something adrift? He stepped over to the lifeline for a closer look. It was a boat following alongside the ship. But what was it doing so close to the ship? There were no running lights, which was not only dangerous, but also illegal. As the dark form pulled up closer to the ship, light from a porthole left carelessly open one level below the seaman suddenly streamed out like a stage spotlight on the water. For an instant, the man at the speedboat's wheel was illuminated. He was in camouflage uniform, his face was blackened, he was armed, and he was looking right at the seaman—smiling.

The seaman and every other man aboard the Eastern Explorer had heard tales of hijackings in this area of the world. He looked forward, then aft anxiously. Where was the sentry? He turned and ran back through the open door into the ship and rushed to an intercommunications phone hanging on the bulkhead. He did not panic. He had trained for this situation countless times. He just had never thought it would ever really happen. And he sure wished he had a weapon, but the engine crew never carried any, unless they were taking part in a drill to repel boarders. This was no drill. He grabbed the phone and pushed the button for the bridge.

Someone on the bridge picked up. "Bridge."

"There's a small boat off the port side, running without lights!" the seaman announced more calmly than he felt. As he listened, he could hear his warning being repeated by the man on the other end of the line, "Captain, there's a boat, port side, without running lights." He realized too late that he should have added the little detail about the armed man in the boat.

The seaman jumped at the sound of three quick explosions from somewhere on the ship. Then he realized the precariousness of his situation. He was unarmed and alone. Still, there had been no general alarm sounded, so perhaps his imagination was playing tricks on him. On the other hand, maybe it wasn't. He looked around for something that might serve as a weapon. As he turned, he stopped suddenly as a dark figure stepped into the open door. His eyes went wide at the sight of the weapon aimed at him.

The impact of the heavy-caliber slug threw him back against the bulkhead. He didn't feel anything. He just thought it odd that he was sitting on the deck in the passageway and couldn't move. And he wondered about the men who were walking past him as if he weren't even there. He wanted to say something, but the words died along with him.

Alarm klaxons finally began to blare throughout the ship, followed by the voice of the bridge watch coming over the loudspeaker system: "All hands on deck to repel boarders! All hands on deck! This is not a drill! All hands on deck." But it was already too late.

On the forward deck, Rudy brought the BAR up and started moving toward the ship's superstructure as he fumbled for the clip. He spotted two armed men in camouflage uniforms coming toward him and ducked behind some heavy cargo tied to the deck for cover.

As the two men came around a corner, he braced the heavy weapon on a crate and tried to insert the clip as quietly as possible. *Now, how do you cock the damn thing?* He thought he figured it out, but wasn't sure it was in correctly as he aimed at the man on the right. He knew for sure, though, these two men were definitely not part of the crew, they were armed, and they had to be pirates. Twenty years in the navy, and he was far from prepared for the fine art of ambushing someone. He wasn't positive he could pull the trigger.

His mind was made up for him as the cold barrel of an AK47 assault rifle touched the side of his head. He glanced up at the man, who he knew was Filipino. He also knew the man had to be Moro. *I am screwed*, he thought, as he lowered the BAR to the deck.

Two more of the ship's enlisted men, whose task it was to pass out firearms from the weapons locker during normal drills, had realized there was no time for formalities. They broke the gun locker open, grabbed as many weapons as they could carry, and then rushed up to the bridge, where they quickly handed out the pistols and automatic rifles to the officers and crewmen.

In a small cubicle just off the bridge, a red headed, freckle-faced Irishman, Danny O'Bannon, who served as the ship's radioman, held the microphone with two shaking hands to keep from dropping it as he sent his first emergency message. He prayed that someone, anyone, might hear it. His voice trembled: "Mayday! Mayday! Mayday! This is the Eastern Explorer. We are being boarded by heavily armed men five miles off the coast of Zamboanga City, Mindanao. We are resisting and have taken casualties. This is—"

Everyone on the bridge was startled when the door that led out to the starboard bridge wing clanged open and several guerrillas stepped in with their weapons trained on the crew. The quartermaster, a boy of nineteen, reacted as he had a hundred times before during his forays on paintball fields. It was a move that had gained him recognition as one of the deadliest opponents in the sport. There was just one minor problem and he realized it the instant he made his move— this wasn't paintball. And the man in front of him wasn't playing as he put a bullet through the boy's heart.

O'Bannon looked over his shoulder and saw his friend fall. He turned back to his radio, "This is Eastern Explorer, near Zamboanga—"

The bridge crew recoiled in horror at the explosion of automatic fire that shredded the affable Irishman and his equipment. The guerrilla who killed both the quartermaster and O'Bannon turned slowly and aimed the still smoking assault rifle at the remainder of the bridge crew. They raised their hands in surrender.

"No! Why, my God! Why?" Captain Blackwell shouted desperately.

One of the guerrillas stepped forward. Blackwell towered over the Filipino. "Captain, you and your crew are now prisoners of the Moro Islamic Liberation Front," the MILF leader said formally. "Where is this ship headed?"

Blackwell could not speak. The guerrilla leader waited a moment. "Captain." he started to repeat his question.

"Manila," Blackwell said, as if from the depths of a trance.

"Your cargo?"

Blackwell tried to focus on the smaller man. "Building materials," he finally was able to say.

"What is in the cargo hold?"

"The same. Building materials."

The guerrilla noticed a quick look between the captain and the executive officer. He turned and whispered to one of his men. The man stepped outside the bridge and a moment later came back in with the steward, Carlos. From his casual, almost jovial demeanor, it was obvious Carlos was friendly with the guerrillas. The look on the captain's face showed surprise and disappointment. "Carlos?" he said in dismay at the betrayal.

The guerrilla leader spoke to Carlos in their native Tagalog, "The captain says they are carrying only building materials."

Carlos eyed Blackwell. "That is all I have seen," he answered back in Tagalog. "But they keep one room locked. I think there is something of great value in there."

The leader turned to a teenage guerrilla with deep pockmarks on his face and motioned to the ship's executive officer. "Take this one below and see what is there," he said. "Take two men with you."

"Yes, sir," the boy said.

The guerrilla leader turned back to Carlos. "Show them the way."

Carlos nodded in abeyance and led the way off the bridge. The teenage guerrilla shoved the executive officer roughly through the door and out onto the bridge wing.

Several decks below, Carlos led them through a passageway. Behind him, the teenager continued to shove the executive officer with a rifle butt in the back until they came to a locked door. Carlos looked at the executive officer and held out his hand.

"I don't have the key," the executive officer protested.

The teenager looked at Carlos, who translated what the executive officer said, and then added, "He's lying."

Without warning or even a threat of harm if he did not cooperate, the teenager's expression never changed as he pivoted and swung his rifle up and hit the officer savagely in the side of the head, nearly knocking him unconscious. The officer staggered and fell to his knees. The teen brought the rifle up again to strike the officer. Carlos held up his hand to stop the boy. He held out his hand to the officer, whose left eye was already swelling shut.

A moment later, the door swung open and the teenager pushed the executive officer into the massive cargo hold. They could see several rows of lumber stacked over twenty feet high. There were pallets of cinder blocks, cement, and rebar. They walked between the aisles of building materials until they came to another locked door.

"The key please, sir," Carlos said, again holding out his hand to the officer.

"I don't have it."

The teenager started to bring up his weapon again. The officer staggered back and tried to protect his face with his arm and pleaded, "No, I really don't have it. The door was locked before we left port. It can only be unlocked at our final destination."

"Which is not Manila, I take it," Carlos said.

The officer didn't answer. Carlos took a pistol from the teenage guerrilla's belt, pulled back the slide to chamber a round, and pointed it at the officer's face.

"Where?"

The officer eyed the gun and swallowed, "Ireland," he muttered, feeling as if he had just betrayed his captain and the rest of the crew.

Carlos did not bother to hide his surprise as he lowered the gun. He studied the officer. "Ireland?" Then he turned and shot the lock off the door.

It was not a smart thing, considering they were standing in a room made entirely of steel. The lock was blown off and pieces of the shattered bullet ricocheted off a rounded edge of the door. One miniscule piece struck the teenager in the temple. The boy looked at Carlos in amazement at the absurdity of his shooting a lock off a steel door, not realizing he was mortally wounded. His brain shut down like a video screen being shut off and the light went out of his eyes. He dropped like a wet rag and his AK47 clattered across the deck.

Carlos looked down with curiosity at the dead boy, shook his head at the whimsy of death, then opened the door and motioned with the gun for the officer to step through. He picked up the AK47 and followed the officer into the storage room.

Inside the second cargo hold there were several large square objects covered by heavy green canvas tarps. Carlos motioned with the AK47 for the officer to pull up one of the tarps, revealing stacks of stainless steel cases. On each was the black and yellow symbol—a three-bladed propeller within a circle—signifying radioactive materials, with the source of origin stenciled below: Department of Atomic Energy, Government of Australia. Carlos grinned and dropped the tarp, and motioned for the officer to leave the room.

8

The sun was an hour from setting. Sixteen surviving Eastern Explorer crewmen were lined up along the ship's railing. Each man stared out across the sea. Eight Moros were behind them and two stood at the railing. A section of the railing had been removed, opening the deck up to the sea.

Captain Blackwell glared defiantly at the guerrilla leader and Carlos as they paraded in front of him and his crew. Rudy was determined not to show any emotion that would give satisfaction to their tormentors. Standing next to him a young sailor whimpered and was near collapsing. The ship's crew knew their imminent fate as each held a cinder block in his hands, with a wire cable that ran from the block and looped around his neck.

The guerrilla leader nodded to Carlos, who walked in front of the prisoners. He smiled at Captain Blackwell, who glared down at him with contempt.

"Any last words before you—" he paused for the dramatic effect as he smiled and motioned toward the water. "Walk the plank, Captain?"

"You are a contemptible coward and a traitor," Blackwell said. "There will be a corner of hell for you and your kind."

Carlos grinned up at Captain Blackwell. "So British. So traditional, to the end." He deftly flipped open a long Filipino butterfly knife then he stepped behind Captain Blackwell and poked him in the back with the sharp blade, and nudged him toward the edge. "Another tradition just for you and your crew, captain. Time to walk the plank."

Carlos stood at Blackwell's side and poked him again with the knife. Blackwell stepped forward involuntarily. He teetered on the edge of the deck. The toes of his shoes dangled over thin air. Carlos leaned forward and whispered in the officer's ear, "Think of me on your way down, infidel."

Blackwell looked down at Carlos and spit in his face, just as the small man shoved the knife in his back. Blackwell fought to keep his balance, but with the cinder block in his hands, it was futile. He pitched over, fell twenty feet to the water, and was gone.

Carlos wiped the spit from his face, turned, and winked at Rudy. "Next."

Rudy was determined not to give the Filipino the satisfaction of seeing him cower, or be forced over the side. Instead, he did something very uncharacteristic for him—he started to curse the Filipino guerrillas, their families, and their entire ancestral line.

This amused Carlos and he started to laugh at the crazy little Guamanian. He turned to look at the two men standing where Captain Blackwell had just been forced over and they too began to laugh.

Rudy continued to rant and one of the men made a sign that the Guamanian must be insane. Rudy then did the second thing very much uncharacteristic for him. He screamed like a banshee and charged at the two men. He ran to the right of one and tossed the cinder block to the left of the other—then he hurled himself over the side, the wire cable that ran from his neck to the cinder block took the two Moros with him. The terrified duo screamed all the way down to the water's surface. And all the way down, Rudy thought, *at least I'm taking two of the sons-of-- bitches with me.*

9

The ship's heavy mooring lines ran down from the Eastern Explorer's bow and stern and were tied around the trunks of ancient trees that hugged the banks of the inland waterway near a remote fishing village. The villagers carried the building materials and anything else that could be taken from the ship down the gangway and along a path lit by torches to waiting stake-bed trucks lined up to take the cargo away. A large covered truck sat apart from the others.

To the destitute fishermen, who cast off from these shores each morning to catch whatever they could in order to feed their hungry families, the Eastern Explore was a major catch. Several members of the MILF group that had taken her and killed the crew lived here and fished from their tiny boats by day then plundered passing ships by night. So, much of the bounty, in the form of the building supplies, would eventually find its way into the villagers' hands to be sold on the lucrative black market. And what wasn't sold, they reasoned, could be used in the village to repair the mosque that had been damaged during the last monsoon season. They saw no incongruity in this line of reasoning. They did not think of the men who had died at sea. It was just part of the way they conducted business. At least for some it was. The leaders of the MILF, on the other hand, were dedicated to their cause and they looked at their days work as a means to an end—to rid the world of unbelievers.

Using dollies, Carlos directed some of the guerrillas loading the stainless steel cases that contained the spent nuclear fuel rods into the back of the truck. The MILF leader came down the gangway and walked over to the men as the last piece of equipment was loaded.

"Send our Somalian brothers up to the bridge," he ordered in Tagalog.

"Yes, sir," Carlos said.

Later, on the bridge, the MILF leader turned as two emaciated Somalians, both members of the Al-Ittihad Al-Islamia, stepped inside. He spoke to them in Arabic, "Do you have everything you need?"

The taller of the two answered, "Yes."

"Good," the MILF leader said, pleased at the prospect of these two men carrying out an invaluable component of his plan. "Allah Akbar, my brothers."

"Allah Akbar, brother," both answered in unison.

The three men embraced and kissed one another on both cheeks, and then the MILF leader left the bridge.

10

CIA Fact Book: *The Spratly Islands consist of more than 100 small islands or reefs. They are surrounded by rich fishing grounds and potentially by gas and oil deposits. They are claimed in their entirety by China, Taiwan, and Vietnam, while portions are claimed by Malaysia and the Philippines. About 45 islands are occupied by relatively small numbers of military forces from China, Malaysia, the Philippines, Taiwan, and Vietnam. Brunei has established a fishing zone that overlaps a southern reef, but has not made any formal claim.*

The Eastern Explorer sailed west of Sin Cowe Island, in the midst of the Spratly Islands. The area had seen numerous military skirmishes between Chinese and Vietnamese naval forces that clashed at Johnson Reef, as well as a buildup of fortifications on several of the small islands.

She had a new name on her fantail, Maartensdijk. A hasty paint job had been made along the ship's superstructure to change her appearance. It might have fooled someone from a distance, but not close up. However, no one would be getting close enough to the ship to make the distinction. Not if the two Somalians could help it.

As teenagers desperate for gainful employment of any kind and regular meals, nineteen-year-old Abdelahi, and his fifteen-year-old brother, Korfa, had joined Somalia's northern clans in the overthrow of Mohamed Siad Barre in 1991. They were siblings and brothers-in-arms, who had left their rat-infested home in the Nugaal region, as well as their widowed mother and their three sisters to take up the fight. They had been drifting aimlessly through the streets of Mogadishu in search of their next victim or their next meal, whichever came first, when they were recruited by one of their many uncles into the Al-Ittihad Al-Islamia movement.

Al-Ittihad Al-Islamia differed from the other Islamic movements in Somalia in that it had its own armed forces and unlike the other radical factions, inclusion was not based on belonging to any particular clan. A willingness to kill indiscriminately, however, was looked upon favorably.

Operating as an Islamic fundamentalism organization, Al-Ittihad Al-Islamia remained a stumbling block to all peace and national reconciliation efforts in Somalia. Its international link to world terrorism was confirmed in an interview in the London-based Arab newspaper, Al-Quds al-'Arabi, by no one of less stature than the world's number one terrorist, Osama Bin Laden, after which SEAL Team Six tracked him down in Pakistan and killed him.

Since the formation of the Transitional Federal Government (TFG) in October 2004, fighting between terrorists and counter-terrorist operatives in Mogadishu had entered into a more lethal stage that threatened to force the country even further towards jihadism and extremist violence.

Now the movement had spread to the South China Sea, thanks to the two brothers.

Deep inside the ship, Abdelahi opened the last battered green box. Stenciled in white letters on its side was the military designation, MIL-C-45010A. He unwrapped the olive-drab cellophane and took out foot-long bar of the white rubbery plasticized mass. He began to knead it as he had seen his mother knead dough for bread. When it was just right, he shaped it into several bricks of C-4 plastic explosives, inserted a blasting cap, ran a wire from it over to a cell phone, which was taped to a 50-gallon barrel of stolen jet fuel oil that the Moros had stored in the most forward space in the bow of the ship. A single stainless steel crate of the radioactive rods sat in the center of the cavernous room. He ran wire from the explosives on the hull to the crate and connected it to the C-4. His younger brother was similarly busy wiring the engine room with more explosives.

When Abdelahi was done, he returned to the bridge and stepped up to the wheel. He disengaged the automatic pilot, looked out through the front windows, and saw what he had been hunting for on the horizon. He pushed a button on a two-way radio as a signal to his brother. A few minutes later, Korfa joined him on the bridge. Abdelahi nodded in the direction of the cruise ship ahead of them.

11

The Bali Song Flower had left Hong Kong a week ago on a forty-five day grand tour of the South China Sea and Sulu Archipelago. She had left Manila the previous day and was now cruising a leisurely twelve knots through the Spratly Islands, and was carrying three thousand passengers and a crew of over nine hundred. The passengers—mostly wealthy Europeans and retired Americans who were here to escape the harsh winter that was now ravaging both continents—baked on the decks, played blackjack in the casino, jogged on the sports deck, swam laps in the speed pool, swooped down a twisting water slide, or listened to a jazz quartet in one of the eight lounges.

On the cruise ship's bridge, the crew went through the motions of keeping the computerized twenty thousand ton, one thousand ninety-five foot long liner on course. A Norwegian officer looked at the radar screen and saw a green blip dead ahead. He went over to the port window and searched with his binoculars until he spotted a vessel. It was coming straight at them.

Where the hell did he learn navigation? He called out to the man at the ship's wheel, "Helmsman, come right rudder, zero one zero." He studied the other ship's position again. "Give him plenty of room." He continued to watch the other ship and muttered, "A million square miles of open water..." But something wasn't right. He lowered the binoculars. "Helmsman, I thought I told you to come right zero one zero."

"I did, sir. He turned into us again," the helmsman said, his confusion evident on his face. "What the hell is he up to?" the captain quizzed no one in particular, then he ordered, "Full right rudder, now!"

"Full right rudder, sir!" the helmsman replied as he spun the wheel hard right, unable to take his eyes off the ship that continued to come straight at them.

Passengers were caught off balance by the sudden listing as the liner struggled to turn out of the path of the other ship. Water sloshed out of the Olympic-sized pool. A boy and girl who were climbing a fake rock wall swung out wildly. Then some of the passengers began to notice the other ship.

The entire bridge crew stared out the window in shocked fascination as the ship bore down on them. No matter how many times the officer ordered a change in course, the cargo ship changed direction and continued on its course straight at the Bali Song Flower.

One of the lookouts on the bridge wing studied the other ship through his binoculars. His view shifted from the bow to the side of the ship, where he saw her name, Maartensdijk, painted in rough letters. Then he looked at the bridge, where he could see a tall black man in a camouflage uniform and wearing a red beret. The man was looking back, seemingly right at him. The lookout started to shout a warning, but it was drowned out by the call from the bridge over the loudspeaker, "Sound the danger signal!"

Six loud blasts from the ship's horn echoed across the water as the space between the two ships continued to close. The blaring warning signal got all of the passengers' and the rest of the crew's attention. They lined up against the railing, mesmerized at the sight of the approaching ship. None seemed to realize the imminent danger speeding toward them. But as the distance between the ships continued to close and the blasts from the horn became more frantic, it was as if the same thought went through their collective consciousness—they had to get away. But, of course, there was no place to go.

By now, it was obvious to everyone on the bridge that a collision was unavoidable. The officer commanded, "Sound the collision alarm! Close all watertight doors throughout the ship!"

Collision alarms sounded on all decks. The crew shut and secured the watertight doors, trapping terrified passengers throughout the ship. On the bridge, the crew appeared to be in a stupor as the other ship closed the last few feet on its collision course.

"Brace for collision!" the officer shouted as he exchanged a look of acceptance of the inevitable with the helmsman. They grabbed for anything solid, and waited the last few, agonizing moments.

The Somalian brothers watched impassively as the giant cruise ship's form filled the windows in front of them. An instant before impact, they turned to each other and embraced, which was not common in their Islamic culture.

"Good-bye, little brother. May Allah welcome you," Abdelahi said in their native Somali.

"And may you be by my side in heaven, my brother," Korfa said softly just as the Eastern Explorer's bow slammed into the side of the Bali Song Flower, cutting a deep gash into the liner.

Tearing metal and screams signaled the death throes of the cruise ship and those aboard her. Muffled explosions deep inside the Bali Song Flower quickly followed. Throughout the liner, terrified passengers were thrown about as if paper dolls cast in the wind. Fires erupted in passageways on every deck. Passengers and crew trapped between watertight doors beat their fists desperately on the doors, pleading for help that would never come. They quickly succumbed to the poisonous black smoke that bellowed up from the fires and through the passageways

As the Eastern Explorer stopped its forward penetration of the Bali Song Flower, the two ships drifted as if in a ghastly lover's embrace. Abdelahi raised a cell phone and pushed the talk button.

Inside the crushed bow, the other cell phone rang. Then the bricks of C-4 detonated, ripping into the fuel drums. The flames vaporized the spent nuclear rods and a fiery maelstrom rushed up and through both ships, consuming everyone in the time it took a child in her mother's arms to take a single breath.

The charred, twisted remains no longer resembled the luxury liner or the old freighter. The ghastly crucifix of burning metal and flesh groaned in agony and began to sink. Soon, all that was left on the surface was smoke, burning debris, melted plastic, and thousands of bodies—the dead and those who would die.

12

Inside the Nebraska Avenue Center offices of the Department of Homeland Security, Eric Stone, Secretary of Homeland Security, and John Langella, Under Secretary of Emergency Preparedness and Response, walked grimly down a long hallway.

"Survivors?" Stone asked. Stone had served as prosecutor in Tallahassee, then as a judge on the Eleventh Circuit Court, before the president nominated and the Senate confirmed him as the third Secretary of Homeland Security, following Michael Chertoff, after he had returned to the private sector.

Langella studied the radio message in the red folder with white lettering, TOP SECRET. "Fifteen, maybe twenty, at the most," he said.

Stone was stunned. "So few?"

As they approached the Command Information Center (CIC), Langella opened a door. "I'm afraid so, Mr. Secretary." They entered CIC where the only sound heard was the air conditioning and people typing on wireless keyboards.

"How many were onboard the cruise ship?" Stone said, as they entered a smaller soundproof room filled with small flat screen panels on every desk and several forty-two inch screens on the far wall.

Langella quickly checked one of the flat screens. A diagram of the Bali Song Flower appeared at the touch of a key. He changed screen shots and the ship's statistics appeared. He scanned down until he came to the crew complement. "The Bali Song Flower was one of seven ships home ported in Hong Kong that cruise the South China and Sulu Sea routes," he said. "Each typically carries three thousand passengers and a crew of more than nine hundred."

Stone shook his head in amazement. "My God!"

Around them, the flat screens on the walls were displaying various hot spots that Homeland Security was monitoring 24/7 around the world. Ten young and extremely focused male and female technologists-analysts were busy operating Ultra-secret cryptography computers. These powerful computers employed linguistic and mathematical techniques to aid the technologists-analysts in converting encrypted information that the governments or organizations they were monitoring had transformed into incomprehensible forms back to readable formats.

"Where are they now?" Stone asked Langella.

"They're still on the Port Royal," he said as he brought up an image of the USS Port Royal, a guided missile cruiser. "Luckily, it was headed for a port call at Ho Chi Minh City."

"Anything on satellite that can explain how this happened"

Langella shook his head, "No, nothing but a lot of empty ocean. For the most part, there's nothing but uninhabited islands in that part of the world. There aren't any satellites assigned to monitor the area on a regular basis."

"We're talking millions of square miles," Stone sat heavily in one of the chairs in front of a monitor. "Yet a cruise liner with over three thousand people aboard and a freighter somehow manage to collide."

Langella touched the shoulder of Gary Lasky, one of the young operatives. Lasky looked up from his screen. "What have you heard from the Port Royal?"

"Not much, sir," Lasky said. "The ship's doctor sent out a preliminary update on the survivors. Most are badly burned. Two more died soon after they were brought aboard."

"Any new intel on the other vessel?"

"Nothing yet, Mr. Secretary."

"Okay," Stone checked the man's nametag, "Agent Lasky, I want to know right away when you hear anything from the Port Royal," Stone said. "Especially if they find a surviving crewmember of the Bali Song Flower. Maybe they can give us some idea of how this happened."

"Yes, sir. Will do," Lasky said, as he turned back to his screen.

Later, Stone and Langella stepped out into the hall. Stone looked at his watch. "I have to report to the president at fourteen hundred. He's going live on the evening news. Get me something to give to him."

"Yes, Mr. Secretary. I'll keep you posted."

"I want to know if this was a horrible accident—or something else."

Stone marched in his retired marine's pace down the hall as Langella went back into CIC.

13

Home ported in Pearl Harbor, USS Port Royal (CG 73) was the twenty-seventh and last of the Ticonderoga-class Aegis cruisers built in the twentieth century. Commissioned in Savannah, Georgia, July 9, 1994, she was also the first of her class to carry women as part of the crew of thirty-three officers and three hundred sixty-seven enlisted.

The Ticonderoga-class cruisers were highly sophisticated warships originally designed to counter the serious air and missile threat that Soviet air and naval forces posed to U.S. carrier battle groups and other task forces.

After the implosion of the Soviet Union and the nearly total abandonment of its navy, Port Royal and her Yokosuka-based, older sister ships, USS Cowpens (CG 63) and USS Chancellorsville (CG 62), were relegated to the WESTPAC duty, where their primary mission was to track the secretive maneuvers of North Korea's submarines. It was no longer their old nemesis, the Soviet Union Navy, but the subs they chased were, for the most part, old, diesel-powered, Russian-built Romeo and Whiskey coastal patrol submarines better suited as museum displays. The North Koreans also had Chinese-designed Sang-O infiltration submarines, each with a crew of nineteen, plus six swimmers, whose job it was to infiltrate and spy on South Korea. As obsolete as the subs were, the Falkland Island War had demonstrated that a small, tactically ineffective submarine force could still have an impact on combat operations simply by being at sea and staying hidden, which the North Koreans were very good at doing.

The day following the mass murder of three thousand innocent travelers, the Port Royal's sickbay overflowed with injured survivors from the Bali Song Flower. Surgeon and Naval Reservist, Lieutenant Commander Steven Chesser, would not normally have been aboard the 567-foot cruiser, because, under normal circumstances, it only rated only an enlisted corpsman or a warrant officer. But these were not normal circumstances. He had been flown over to the Port Royal on one of its two LAMPS 3, SH-60 Sea Hawks from the nuclear-powered aircraft carrier, USS Abraham Lincoln (CVN-72).

Navy surgeon, LCDR Chesser hovered over a badly burned boy he guessed to be about ten-years-old as he used tweezers and gently removed the burned remains of a GAP T-shirt from the blisters that covered most of the child's back. An IV carried a constant stream of morphine to the boy, as he struggled bravely not to cry, but tears filled his blue eyes. At another steel bunk, Hospital Corpsman Second Class Gabriel Pace washed the deep chest lacerations and burns of the boy's mother. Fortunately, she was unconscious.

"How's she doing, Petty Officer Pace?" Chesser asked without looking up from the boy.

Pace glanced over at the boy. "I don't think it's as bad as it looks, sir. No broken bones and I can suture up the lacerations pretty much," he said. "I figure she's around thirty-percent covered with second degree burns."

The door to sickbay opened and the ship's executive officer, or XO, Commander Diane Macina, stepped in. She was dressed from head to toe in a white HAZMAT suit. She carried the hood in her arms.

"Steve?"

Chesser didn't look up at her as he sprayed the boy's back with saline solution. "XO."

"We've got a problem," she said, the tone clearly serious.

"Now what?" He asked wearily. Then he looked up at her and noticed what she was wearing.

Suddenly, an alarm began to blare. It was immediately followed by a warning over the ship's 1MC, the internal communications speaker system. From the bridge, the petty officer of the watch announced, "Decontamination wash down is underway. All non-essential topside personnel report to sickbay and remain below decks."

Chesser shook his head in resignation and looked at Pace. "It's going to get real crazy around here, real fast."

"I'll break out what we'll need," Pace said as he went over to one of the supply cabinets.

The warning continued to come over the 1MC, "Hazmat personnel report to duty stations immediately. Damage control set Circle William throughout the ship."

Macina glanced at the speaker on the bulkhead as the warning was repeated, then she looked at Chesser. They had known one another since Annapolis. They had both been stationed in San Diego and their kids had gone on trips to Balboa Park together. They both knew that this was very serious and that what they had been training for over the entirety of their careers had just happened. A nuclear weapon of mass destruction had been used and they were at ground zero.

"I'll have some people come down to help you and Petty Officer Pace with the radiation monitoring." She slipped on the protective hood, stepped out into the passageway, and then headed up a ladder to take charge of the decontamination process.

Outside, the entire ship was being coated in a shower of white foam. The men and women who made up the crew were indistinguishable in their HAZMAT suits as the used high-pressure hoses and foam to wash down and decontaminate the ship.

14

Stone hadn't slept for over thirty-six hours and it showed as he looked up from behind his massive mahogany desk when Langella entered his office. Langella placed a top-secret document on Stone's desk. Stone didn't bother to open it. "Give me the short version," he said.

Langella sat down in the leather chair facing Stone. His expression told Stone that he wasn't going to like what Langella had to say. "There are high levels of radiation contamination aboard the Port Royal, as well as the entire area of the collision." Langella glanced at the folder. "One of the survivors from the Bali Song Flower was able to tell Port Royal's ICO that the other ship was the Maartensdijk. But that's not possible."

"Why is that?'

"The real Maartensdijk is an old cargo steamer built in the early nineteen hundreds that, at the time of the collision, was being offloaded in Mubai, India. The Maartensdijk does have a history of its own, though. Last year, it was hijacked by pirates and the crew was left on a small island."

"Pirates?" Stone said. "You're serious?"

"So I'm told."

"Follow this up. Set up a briefing for all concerned department heads, including Spec Ops, ASAP."

Langella stood up to leave. "You think this is a matter for Homeland Security?" he said. "It's a little out of our backyard, Mr. Secretary."

"Ever since nine-eleven, the world is our backyard," Stone said, as he picked up the phone. "Set it up."

"Yes, Mr. Secretary. I'll let you know when everyone's dialed in," Langella said, as he turned and left.

Stone bushed a button on the phone for his secretary, "I need to talk to the president—right away." He hung up.

15

Jamal Karami-Hakkak had made millions in the booming Florida real estate market over the last five years. As he had been instructed during his training in Afghanistan, he obediently deposited a major portion of his riches in four Grand Cayman accounts used to finance the Mujahideen-e-Khalq, a Marxist Iranian resistance movement. The portion he held back for himself was more than sufficient to assure that he, his wife and two daughters, as well as his mistress lived in a lavish style to which he had quickly grown accustomed and felt he deserved.

On this night, he was behind the wheel of his brand new, two-hundred thousand dollar, thirty-four foot, black and red Phantom racing boat. He slowly throttled down the Twin 500 EFI Bravo diesels as the boat approached a deserted stretch of beach on an outcropping of forested land that resembled a whale's tail, on which a rutted, dirt road, Old State Road 4A, ended.

For more than one hundred years, smugglers and poachers had sailed in and out of these waters along the Florida coastline and spent many leisurely nights around campfires on its white beaches boasting of their exploits as they savored spoils of their plundering. However, the men whom Karami-Hakkak was landing on the beach this night were neither poachers nor smugglers. They were al-Qa'ida terrorists.

Because the water was too shallow to allow the boat to land, two of the men hopped out into the water and pulled the boat from either side until the bow eased up on the beach. The others jumped out of the boat and headed toward the dirt road. Karami-Hakkak and another man who he had just met that night stayed in the boat. He pulled back on the throttle and eased the boat out to sea into the darkness.

The six men knelt in tall grass and watched as a vehicle maneuvered toward them along the badly eroded road, its headlights bouncing up and down. As the vehicle drew closer, they saw it was a black Ford Explorer. It pulled off the road into the grass.

The driver and a passenger got out, careful to check up and down the road. Both carried automatic weapons slung on their backs. The driver took out a flashlight and flipped it on and off three times.

After the all-clear signal, the six men stood up and headed through the grass toward the SUV. One of the men shook hands with the driver. The other five men approached the SUV and were just about to climb in when their clandestine world of darkness was brought to light—literally.

Three spotlights blinked on from nearby trees and the eight men around the SUV were suddenly exposed. A fourth light caught Karami-Hakkak in his expensive new toy out in the open. A siren blasted twice from the Coast Guard Patrol Boat, Key Largo, followed by a voice warning over a bullhorn, "This is the U.S. Coast Guard. Stop your motor and raise your hands."

The men standing by the SUV had no intension of raising their hands. They reached for their weapons. Two carried M9 9mm pistols; the others had M4s and MP5 assault rifles. They froze in place as another voice blared at them from behind one of the spotlights, "Drop your weapons right now," it commanded, then added ominously, "This is your only warning!"

The man in the boat with Karami-Hakkak apparently had made up his mind to be a martyr without feeling any compunction to consult with Karami-Hakkak about his decision to sacrifice himself along with the terrorist turned real estate mogul. The man bent down and flipped open a long satchel he had brought aboard the boat earlier, pulled out a rocket-propelled grenade and fired it at the Key Largo. The grenade missed the Coast Guard cutter by only a few feet. The Coast Guard crew opened up with the cutters forward 50-caliber machine guns on the Phantom speedboat.

All of the Phantom's horsepower could not help Karami-Hakkak and the other man as the bullets ripped them and the boat to shreds. In seconds what was left of their bodies and the boat settled to the sandy bottom.

From behind the spotlight, Special Agent for Homeland Security James Parris and his team of ten agents were poised with their weapons trained on the eight men surrounding the SUV. "So much for negotiating a peaceful surrender," Parris muttered. He flipped the safety off his M249 SAWS light machine gun. "Let's try to take at least one of these idiots alive," he said in his wire mike.

The terrorists remained frozen in the bright glare from the spotlights. It was only for a second, but it felt like the moment dragged on forever. Then the SUV driver leaped away from the vehicle and fired at one of the spotlights. It exploded in a shower of glass and a bright burst of flaring light. The other men scattered and opened fire, shooting into the dark in the hopes of hitting one of the agents, or at least causing them to duck for cover so the terrorists might make their escape.

Marine sergeant Max "Stinger" Sand was perched in a tree more than a hundred yards away from the melee. With his .308 M-86, it was an easy shot for him, as he lined up the crosshairs on the driver's head and pulled the trigger. Through the scope, he could see the back of the man's head explode in a shower of blood, brains, and bone.

"Driving SUVs can be detrimental to your health," Sand joked to himself. He moved the rifle slightly right, found the SUV passenger who was firing into the trees and killed him. "You live by the SUV, you die by the SUV, I always say."

Parris shouted into his wire microphone, "Damn it, Stinger! I need a live one. Can't you just wing one for the team?"

Sand squinted through the night-vision scope again. The green world that he saw revealed flashes from all the weapons, which made it difficult at first for him to find a man crawling in the tall grass. Finally, he spotted one crawling toward the nearby woods. Sand moved the crosshairs from the back of the guy's head down to his ass, and whispered into his mike, "One winged rag head coming up, boss." He put the bullet into the man's right buttock and watched through the scope as the man struggled to get up and run, then collapsed. "One stinger delivered, as ordered."

In seconds, the fighting escalated into chaos. Parris shouted into his radio, "S and D, troops."

From seemingly nowhere, tracers crisscrossed, lighting up the grassy area, as the terrorists were determined to fight to the death. Three of them were granted their wishes as the entire team fired into the grass. Two of the men appeared to be more rational as they tossed their weapons aside and threw up their hands to surrender.

A young agent, Gary Wiler, popped up out of the grass near the two and screamed at them, "Down on your bellies! Get down! Now!"

The two acted as if they didn't understand him. Wiler stared at them, not sure what to do, and then he heard Parris' voice come across his headset, "Wiler! I said S and D!"

"They're unarmed," Wiler protested.

"Put them down! Now!" Parris commanded.

The two men looked panic-stricken. The younger of the two looked like he was only about seventeen. He pleaded, "Don't shoot! We surrender."

The second chimed in, "We give up. Please do not shoot."

Wiler glanced over his shoulder and saw Parris and the other members of the team running toward them. Wiler turned back to the two men. He didn't want to kill them, but he would if they did not obey his orders. "You want to live, get down on your knees," he said, wishing the men down. "You want to die right here? Get down. Get your hands behind your backs."

The younger man sank to his knees as Parris approached. The others spread out behind him. Wiler started toward the two men. He called out to Parris, "It's okay, sir. I got them. They gave up."

Parris strode up behind Wiler, brought up his Glock and put a round through the older man's right ear. The man's body jerked back and fell face-first into the grass. Parris shifted the Glock to the younger man, who at the sight of his comrade being summarily executed, dropped to his belly and begged, "No, please don't kill me!"

Parris calmly shot him between the shoulder blades. The young man grunted and tried to reach behind his back. Wiler stared in shock. Parris gave Wiler a disgusted look, and then he put another bullet into the young man's back. The man stopped moving.

Parris slipped the Glock under his jacket and turned to Wiler. "When I give you a direct order, I expect you to obey it. Without hesitation!" It was no more than a whisper, but it was like a thunderclap to Wiler.

"He was just a kid and he was unarmed," Wiler accused.

Parris glared at Wiler. "Unarmed." He looked down at the two dead men, and then nodded to agent Mike Jackson. Jackson jumped down into the swampy area next to the bodies. He gave the bodies a cursory examination, and then looked up knowingly.

"Real careful, Mike," Parris warned.

"Wouldn't have it any other way," Jackson said as he knelt down beside the younger man's body. He took more time, looked the body over very carefully. As he lifted the back of the young man's Miami Dolphins jacket ever so slightly, he spotted the glint of a thin wire running from under the man's jacket down to where it was wrapped around the man's right thumb. Jackson eased a razor-sharp knife out of his boot and slipped it beneath the jacket material. He gingerly cut a slit up the back of the lightweight material until the jacket split opened like a halved chicken. He put the knife away and eased the two halves of the jacket apart, exposing a belt of C-4 wrapped around the man's back.

The other agents saw the explosive belt. Wiler closed his eyes for a long moment, realizing how stupid he had been and that if it had not been for Parris taking control of the situation, he and several of his team members would already be dead. He forced himself to look up at Parris.

"We get back to base, turn in your gear," Parris said coolly. "You're off the team."

Wiler looked crushed at the command, but he knew, as much as he hated it, that Parris was right. Dejected, he started up to the road.

Parris felt the vibration of his cell phone and snapped it open. "Parris." He listened a moment, then motioned to Jackson, "Wrap it up."

Jackson gave him a little salute with an index finger, "Right, boss."

Parris headed toward the black Ford Explorer that the dead terrorists would no longer need. As he passed Wiler, Parris grabbed him by the coat sleeve. "Get me to the airfield in ten minutes and maybe, just maybe, you'll keep your job."

A look of hope crossed Wiler's face. "Yes, sir," he said, trying not to show too much enthusiasm. Wiler jumped behind the wheel of the Explorer and had it moving at high speed along the dirt road before Parris could fasten his seat belt.

16

A small fishing boat cruised a few miles off Mindanao. Aboard the ancient craft, the Filipino fishermen struggled to pull aboard a heavy net. Something heavy forced the men to put their backs into pulling the net over the side onto the boat. Fish flopped over the deck as a ten-year-old boy swept them into the cargo hold. The rest of the catch cascaded onto the deck, consisting of crabs, squid — and the decomposing bodies of three men.

The boy looked down at what was left of Rudy Carbullido, whom he did not know. But he did recognize the two others snared by the wire that ran from the stranger's neck to the cinder block. They were men from his village who took part in the capture of the Eastern Explorer.

17

Eleven agents from various divisions of Homeland Security and two foreign governments were gathered around the long black oval table in the large conference room. Agent Parris quickly scanned the room, as was his habit. Even in this room, probably one of the safest and most secure in the world, he had a need to know every escape route. Attention to such details had saved his life on more than on occasion.

He knew a few of the others and they exchanged quick glances. He noticed a tall, bearded Indian studying him. But he was not as brazen as the American, who was studying him.

Everyone looked up as Secretary Stone and Langella entered.

"Please, everyone take your seats," Stone said.

As they slipped into their seats, Langella went to the front of the room. A flat screen monitor slid silently down from the ceiling. A photo of the Eastern Explorer came up on the screen. Langella hit the play button on a tape recorder. They heard the excited voice of the ship's radioman, "Mayday! Mayday! Mayday! This is Eastern Explorer! We are being boarded by heavily armed pirates…"

Parris and a couple of the other agents exchanged looks at the mention of pirates. The radioman's voice continued, "…five miles off the coast of Zamboanga City, Mindanao. We are resisting. We have taken casualties. This…"

A metallic clang interrupted the radioman's urgent call for help, then he tried to finish, "…is the Eastern Explorer…"

An explosion ripped from the Bose speakers startling most at the table, but one of the women was clearly disturbed by the sound of machine gun fire, followed by the cry of pain as the radioman was murdered. Then there was the static, which was even more ominous than the sounds of carnage that preceded it.

Langella turned the machine off and motioned to a refined looking Englishman. "At this time, I would like to introduce Sir Thomas Burkenshire, of the International Maritime Organization," he said.

The tall, slightly stooped Englishman, who had appeared a few days before on the BBC broadcast concerning the battle that took place between the Indian commandos and the pirates that had hijacked the freighter near the entrance of the Strait of Malacca, stood stiffly as Langella took his seat. In his eighties, a lifetime of competing in all nature of sports, back country treks, expeditions onto every major mountain range on the planet, and having served on the front lines of two wars—being severely wounded in one—had taken its toll on his body. As he walked stiffly, aided by an elaborately carved cane with a sterling handle, up to the podium, he gave an almost unperceptive nod to Captain Vajpayee.

A polished speaker, Lord Burkenshire maintained eye contact with various members as he spoke, "Ladies. Gentlemen. As you know the IMO, formerly known as the Maritime Safety Committee, has the unique mission for the twenty-first century of tracking and, we hope, capturing or killing members of the various pirate organizations around the world," he said. He motioned to the flat screen monitor. A pie chart graphic came up on the flat screen behind him.

"According to the Piracy Reporting Center," he paused for affect, "which is headquartered in Kuala Lumpur, there were three hundred forty-four reported incidents of piracy and armed robbery on the high seas worldwide, last year." He pointed to the pie chart that showed a disproportionate number of ships were attacked in Indonesia and the Malacca Straights. "In the first quarter of this new year, one hundred thirty-eight vessels were boarded in the Strait of Malacca, alone. Fifteen ships were hijacked, six of which have yet to be recovered. Over two hundred thirty-eight crewmembers were taken hostage to be ransomed, and another sixty-seven, as we've just heard an example of, were brutally murdered.

"We believe that these numbers, as disturbing as they are, do not fully represent the true cost in money and lives. Fully half or more of the attacks go unreported because ship owners worry that the costs of disclosure outweigh the benefits. They do not want incidents reported because investigations will delay shipments and increase insurance premiums, not to mention make it more difficult to find crews willing to sail their vessels."

One of the women, Senator Jacqueline Green, whose grandmotherly appearance belied an inner, hardnosed, dedicated bureaucrat who was presently serving as the new chairperson of the Special Senate Select Committee on Anti-Terrorism, leaned forward. "Sir Burkenshire," she said.

He smiled, "Please, Thomas."

She ignored his attempt at informality. "Sir Burkenshire, are we talking primarily about small inter-island ferries and coastal fishing boats?" she asked, revealing to more than one person in the room that she was definitely not up to speed for her new job. "Is this really anything more than a regional problem concerning scattered incidents of common thieves and hijackers committing armed robberies and kidnappings? Isn't this more of a local police matter than a Homeland Security concern?"

Burkenshire, always the Englishman and never one to upbraid a lady, no matter how ill informed she might be, pushed a button and a photo of the cruise ship Bali Song Flower. "I am sure that everyone in this room is well aware of the fact that the media has been reporting that the collision between the Bali Song Flower and the Martensdijk was an unfortunate accident," he said.

Another image came up behind him. It was a black and white photo of a Manila Times' news story about a band of guerrillas in a jungle setting. They were masked and heavily armed, as they stood threatening over an obviously terrified family that a caption identified as American missionaries from California that were being held for ransom.

Parris eyed the image. He remembered the family, as well as the terrorists.

"We have received confirmation only this morning that this cold-blooded murder of more than three thousand souls was the work of the extremist group, Abu Sayyaf, or ASG. We believe they were assisted by at least two members of the Somalian Al-Ittihad Al-Islamia. The point I want to make is the degree of planning that went into the sinking of the Bali Song Flower and how it relates to recent hijackings."

"The ASG are thugs who make a living extorting their own people or kidnapping foreigners to finance their movement," Parris said. "If there wasn't any money in it for them, why sink the Bali Song Flower?

Burkenshire looked at Parris. "I'm sorry, we haven't been introduced."

"Special Agent James Parris," Parris said.

Lord Burkenshire turned slowly and studied the photo for a long moment, then back at Parris in recognition. "It was you who brought out the Randolph family," he said, not bothering to disguise his admiration. Yes, I've heard of your, shall we say, colorful reputation for taking matters to the extreme."

Parris said confidently, "These are extreme times, Sir Burkenshire, that call for extreme measures. These people only understand one thing, the business end of a weapon."

"You're referring to your 'meeting' with the ASM?" Burkenshire said.

"You could call it that." Parris looked up at the photo behind Burkenshire, and added, ""I had a good team with me," Parris said, then added, "If you're right, and the ASM is aligned with Al-Ittihad Al-Islamia, then the ASM has changed its tactics from financing strictly local efforts and they're going global by linking up with al-Qaeda."

"You can be sure of it," Lord Burkenshire said. "And they were not content with killing only those aboard the Bali Song Flower." He paused a moment as he studied one face in particular. "We have ascertained their objective in another incident was a load of nuclear materials. We believe they have already deployed it as a WMD."

This gets everyone's attention. He used a laser pointer to draw a circle that represented thousands of square miles surrounding the site of the sinking of the Bali Song Flower. "The entire area where the ships went down is hot. And the prevailing winds are spreading the contamination across the nearby Spratly Islands. Although they are, for the most part, uninhabited, there are military garrisons on a number of them. Their governments have been notified and are in the process of evacuating their people at this time. However, easterly winds are spreading the contamination in the direction of Palawan and the Sulu Sea."

"I'm not aware of any reports of missing nuclear materials," said Ernest Volger, a rotund, fashion-challenged analyst. Though he wore the remnants of his breakfast—and perhaps more than one other meal—on his tie, Volger had earned admittance to the room because he headed Homeland Security's Nuclear Incident Response Team, whose role it was to provide expert personnel and specialized equipment in dealing with nuclear terrorism. "Are you saying Abu Sayyaf is in possession of nuclear materials?"

Lord Burkenshire looked back at a man who was visibly squirming in his seat. "I am sure my good friend, Jerome Whitman, who serves as the director of the Australian Nuclear Energy Commission, can shed some light on this," he said.

Whitman had a dear-in-the-headlights look in his eyes, as if he had just been ambushed, which he had. "I don't have any idea what you're talking about, Lord Burkenshire," he said.

Stone stood up and placed both hands on the table as he glared at Whiteman. "Let's cut to the chase, sir," he said bluntly. "We know the Eastern Explorer was carrying spent fuel rods destined for the Sellafield nuclear plant in the UK. The fact that your agency neglected to inform the Philippine government that it was transporting nuclear materials through their waterways is serious enough, but then not to report that it was hijacked is on the verge of international criminality."

Whitman visibly stiffened. "Sir, I can assure you we would have—"

"How long did you intend to wait before letting the rest of the world know that you've lost enough nuclear materials to arm every terrorist organization on the planet?"

"That's a bit of an over statement, sir. And I don't see what the fate of the Eastern Explorer has to do with the Bali Song Flower," Whitman said defensively. Whitman was not a career politician and lying did not come naturally to him, but he tried. "You've said nothing that indicates one has anything to do with the other. And to ask us to believe a ragtag band of common thieves could be responsible is ridiculous. The crew was armed and well trained."

"The Abu Sayyaf is anything but a band of common thieves," Parris interjected. "They are well financed, heavily armed, and determined to destroy the Philippine government and all those who cooperate with the West." Parris didn't care what Whitman, or anyone else in the room thought, as he added, "I don't know how well trained you think the crew was, but I'm willing to bet they weren't expecting to be boarded at night from the stern while underway. And I have yet to meet any sailor, other than American SEALs, who would be equipped and trained well enough to deal with this type of situation."

Whitman's eyes narrowed as he stared at Parris. "How would you know how these alleged attacks are made, agent Parris?"

"That's how I'd do it," Parris said.

Whitman looked indignant. "And I suppose you are one of these—SEALs?"

"Agent Parris' credentials are not up for discussion, sir," Stone said firmly.

"Be that as it may," Whitman blustered. "I still see no evidence that the disappearance of our vessel has any connection with the sinking of the Bali Song Flower."

"If there is, and the guerrillas have her cargo, your company just handed every terrorist in the region, and their allies worldwide, the ability to deliver devastation to millions," Parris said.

"That's a pretty significant leap in logic," Whitman said.

For the first time, Captain Vajpayee spoke up in a clipped, precise British accent, "I totally concur with Agent Parris," he said. "Our own intelligence has uncovered an alliance between the Abu Sayyaf and the Aceh rebels that effectively extends each groups' reach throughout Malaysia. If these two organizations have, which seems highly likely, have joined forces with Al-Ittihad Al-Islamia, they have extended their influence beyond the Pacific and into the Atlantic. If they have secured these nuclear materials, then there is great peril for millions, as well as the potential for contamination of vital fishing and shipping regions for many generations."

Vajpayee realized many in the room did not know who he was. He stood and introduced himself, "Captain Anumita Roy Vajpayee, MCF, Indian Marine Commando Force." He looked over at Parris. "Agent Parris is quite right in his assessment of the Abu Sayyaf. They continue to receive funding and weapons through Al-Qa'ida. They have recently infiltrated and even eliminated a number of pirate organizations. And they have proven to be even more ruthless. They have murdered entire crews, and have even resorted to setting fully laden oil tankers adrift with no regard should they collide with another or run aground and possibly create ecological disasters. We have intelligence that on more than one occasion they have forced tanker crews to instruct them how to maneuver the vessels. All that they took with them were technical papers on the operation of the ships. Not unlike the hijackers of 9/11 who were only interested in learning how to fly the aircraft, these hijackers only want to know how to steer these vessels. The reason is obvious. If there is any possibility of it, we should assume they have gotten their hands on your cargo, and they will not hesitate to use it."

"That is precisely why I have asked Agent Parris and Captain Vajpayee to be present at this meeting," Stone said.

Parris and Vajpayee exchanged a look, as Stone continued, "There will be a joint unit mission to determine if the Abu Sayyaf has the remaining nuclear materials or has already dispersed them."

"If there is a connection between the Eastern Explorer and the Bali Song Flower, what course of action do you propose?" Green asked.

"I propose to kill the bastards and take it back," Parris said.

"That may the ultimate solution, Agent Parris," Green said, "but if you intend to go after these people, don't you think we need to at least inform the Philippine government that American and Indian Special Forces will be invading its territory?"

"Over my dead body," Parris said, as he winked at Vajpayee. "Or my vociferous colleague's dead body."

Vajpayee's eyes narrowed at Parris and he mouthed, "vociferous," back at him. Those around the table looked concerned.

"I might have put it a little more diplomatically," Stone said, as he gave Parris a disproving look, "but Agent Parris states the essence of the situation. We feel that the Philippine government has—for whatever reason—been reluctant to hunt down and destroy the Abu Sayyaf. Therefore, they will be notified when the mission is successfully completed and the teams have been retrieved."

"What if the mission is compromised," Green said.

"It won't be," Parris said to her.

"But what if it is?" she said, resolutely, determined to get a straight answer from Parris.

Parris looked at her as he said slowly, "Then I'll know someone in this room didn't keep his…or her…mouth shut. And the last thing anyone in this room wants is for me to consider them an enemy."

"Is that a threat?"

"I never threaten."

Later, as Parris and Vajpayee walked down the steep granite steps of the Homeland Security building, Vajpayee stopped and offered his hand to Parris.

"If we are going to be breaking untold numbers of international laws together and risking embarrassing both our countries should we be captured or killed in an allied country, perhaps you should call me Roy," he said.

Parris shook his hand. "Well, Roy, we've got less than twenty-four hours to mount up this operation."

"Mount up? Is that something from your days as a cowboy in Wyoming on your father's ranch? I believe he raises Herford cattle and even some of your country's magnificent bison."

Parris studied Roy a moment, and then smiled slightly. "You've been doing your homework, Roy. And they're called buffalo."

"Your techniques are well known—even in Trivandrum."

"The special forces base where you command the Royal Marine Counter Terrorist Strike Force that snuck into Haiphong Harbor, killed fifteen pirates, and sailed the hijacked ship away in broad daylight."

Now it was Roy's turn to smile. "And you do your homework, also."

Parris held out his hand to Roy this time. "Let's go hunt us down some pirates, Roy."

"We call them sea wolves because of their inhumanity and they often hunt in packs."

"Then this will be the hunt of the sea wolves," Parris said as they shook hands.

18

Afghanistan's history has been and continues to be turbulent and prone to violence. In this crossroads of Central Asia, the Afghan people have survived the comings and goings of numerous empire builders, including the Persians, the Mongol hordes united by Genghis Khan, Alexander and his Greek battalions, the British, the Soviets, and now the Americans.

To govern Afghanistan has always been a risky proposition—often fatal—for the man in charge. Over the last century, eleven rulers have been assassinated, executed, deposed, or overthrown. There was one forty-year period, while under the rule of King Zahir Shah, during which the country experienced relative stability. This ended in 1973, when his brother-in-law, Sardar Mohammed Daoud overthrew Shah during one of the few bloodless coups in the region. Those who coveted Daoud's throne, however, were not as obliging. In 1978, the Communist People's Democratic Party of Afghanistan murdered him and his entire family before taking control of the country.

It was at this time that the CIA—under the presidencies of Jimmy Carter and then Ronald Reagan—thought the best course of action was to finance, arm and train a loosely aligned group of opposition fighters known as the mujahideen. Their very name means jihad, or holy warrior. Their latest mission was driving out the current—at that time—empire builders, the Soviets. With the support of the United States, they waged a bloody, take-no-prisoners conflict that lasted ten years, between 1979 and 1989.

When not fighting foreign invaders, the various mujahideen factions turned on one another. Out of chaos order followed, but at a stiff price. Warlords came into power, resulting in a civil war in which more than ten thousand Afghans were killed in the Kabul area alone. The Taliban took control from the warlords in 1996. Initially, the Taliban brought order to the war-torn country and eliminated payments that business people were making to the warlords for protection. The reduction of factional fighting brought about political stability and radical ideology was, at first, viewed as a positive development. The Taliban sought to impose its strict interpretation of Islamic Sharia law on the ninety percent of the country that it controlled, while it gave safe haven to terrorists, particularly al-Qaida.

The Taliban's affiliation with al-Qa'ida was made *official* when the Northern Alliance leader Abdur Rabb ur Rasool Sayyaf personally invited Osama bin Laden to move into the neighborhood and forged an alliance between the Taliban and his al-Qa'ida organization. The relationship between the Taliban and al-Qa'ida was formalized on a personal level when one of bin Laden's sons married the daughter of one of the Taliban's most influential leaders, Mullah Mohammad Omar.

In answer to the al-Qa'ida-backed attack on September 11, 2001, the United States, with the help of the United Kingdom, and a coalition of other countries invaded Afghanistan with the stated intent of removing the Taliban because of its refusal to hand over Osama bin Laden. In fact, though, the Taliban government, which, at that time, was the recognized ruling authority in Afghanistan, did agree to judge bin Laden in an Islamic court, after which, it would hand him over to a neutral country for a war crimes trial. The charade played out as the United States sent the Taliban an ultimatum that included a demand that the Taliban hand over all al-Qaeda leaders and close all terrorist training camps.

Of course, the Taliban refused. The Taliban left Kandahar to regroup along the border between Afghanistan and Pakistan, and continued to recruit new fighters from the madrassahs, Arabic for school, to supplement the more traditional Qur'anic schools that are thought to be the primary breeding ground for new Taliban fighters.

More than a year after the devastating earthquake that struck the valleys beyond

Muazffarabad, the capital of Azad, Kashmir, on October 8, 2005, eighty percent of the mountain

village of Sahr-i-Zārān still lay in ruins. The 7.6 magnitude quake was the most severe in history

to strike the region. Muazffarabad was destroyed, more than seventy-five thousand died and a

half million people in the most remote areas received little or no aid.

The International Committee of the Red Cross (ICRC) conducted a large-scale operation

to evacuate the injured and provide relief supplies. Access roads were impassable, so the ICRC

flew in doctors and ferried out the injured to a makeshift one hundred-bed hospital set up at a

former cricket ground.

ICRC moved on to the next major disaster, leaving a humanitarian void that was partially

filled by the Canadian branch of Läkare i Världen/Médecins du Monde Sweden, whose primary

role was to provide humanitarian relief, reconstruction, and long-term development in rural

Nimruz province. Many of the Canadian activities were supported by volunteers, most of whom

were healthcare professionals. The organization also welcomed other professionals and professed

not to support any political party or religion.

In a perfect world, this non-political positioning may have protected those who came to

help, but the situation in Sahr-i-Zārān was drastically far from perfect. The remains of dirt and

stone huts clung to the side of a steep, craggy mountain. Sickly children lingered in the dusty

streets because the buildings were no longer safe to enter. Women covered from head to toe in

burkas walked in twos and threes to the remnants of a market set up outside the ruins, where

poor farmers sold their stunted vegetables. Throughout the village, bearded men carried on

business, such as it was.

Joshua Parris was far from home and very much alone. He had first come to Afghanistan as a medic with the Army's 75th Ranger Regiment, a light infantry unit out of Fort Benning, Georgia. The regiment had served honorably during World War II, and in Vietnam. It had also taken part in what many thought of as the politically expedient little wars, Operation Urgent Fury, the invasion of Grenada in 1983, and Operation Just Cause in 1989, the invasion of Panama, with the key objective being the capture of its president.

After leaving the army at the end of his second enlistment on the last day of the twentieth century, he planned to attend Johns Hopkins University School of Medicine in Maryland. First, he visited his father at his Wyoming ranch. After two weeks of listening to ranchers' complaining every night at the local saloon about everything from declining beef prices to illegal aliens crossing their lands, he was more than ready to head east.

When he arrived on his brother's doorstep in Virginia, he had another week before his first classes were scheduled to begin. James gave him the nickel tour of CIA headquarters. Then they went for drinks at a bar that catered to cops.

Wherever they went, be it a fast food joint or an upscale pub, the Parris brothers made an impression, particularly with the women. Their tall, ruggedly dangerous good looks would bring female conversation to a halt. This had always been the case. As boys growing up on the ranch, because of their Nordic features, slim waists and broad shoulders, along with their long, sun-bleached blond hair, they were often referred to as the Viking twins. However, the one physical feature that seemed to transfix both women and men were their eyes. Deep set in tanned faces, they were the color of brilliant lavender green, with tiny flecks of yellow and brown. Upon noticing Joshua's eyes aboard a Delta flight, the attendant compared them to her Persian cat's eyes. After the plane landed in Atlanta, he got the chance to meet the feline and, sure enough, he and the cat could have come from the same litter, he joked, as he and the flight attendant settled into her hot tub with drinks.

Joshua began his studies at Johns Hopkins the following week. He had the aptitude, but he soon discovered that he had little in common with the students or faculty. As a former Army Ranger, he saw the day-to-day living experience from an entirely different perspective than his classmates. And as a former medic, he had more *front line* medical experience, including patching up multiple gunshot wounds and saving men who had their legs or faces blown off by roadside IEDs, improvised explosive devices, than many of his instructors.

He made it through the first year of his studies. Then one day at the nearby Burger King, he ran into an Army recruiter. When Joshua noticed the soldier was a Ranger, he struck up a conversation. Upon learning that Joshua had served as a medic with the Rangers, the recruiter nearly tripped over himself to tell Joshua that he could guarantee he would receive a hundred thousand dollar signing bonus, plus his choice of duty stations if he would reenlist. The recruiter explained that the Army needed combat experienced medics. Until that moment, Joshua did not realize just how much he missed being around people who knew the meaning of honor and watching the back of the trooper next to you. He also didn't realize that he really missed the action. He was an action junky.

Because he had only been out of the Army for a little over a year, in which time he had been furthering his professional knowledge by attending medical school, Joshua did not have to go through basic training again and was able to reenlist with the rank of sergeant. And since medics were worth their weight in gold, he also did not have to retake the six-month operator-training course. Instead, he was rushed through an intense four-week refresher course in an isolated corner of Fort Bragg. It was then only a matter of weeks before he found himself back in northern Afghanistan, where he teamed up with a troop of the 1st Special Forces Operational Detachment-Delta (SFOD-D), whose job it was to track down and kill Taliban fighters in the area.

The team stayed clear of the villages for the most part, keeping to the high peaks where they could monitor any movement on the roads below. But an informant told them that the warlord, Abdul Mohammad Mohaqiq, was coming to Sahr-i-Zārān, a village in the team's district, to see one of his sons who had been badly injured when a bomb he was assembling detonated.

Joshua came into the village two days before Mohaqiq's expected arrival. He was posing as a volunteer medical student named Ermanno Grossi and was working with the Läkare i Världen/Médecins du Monde Sweden, an organization that provided medical care to the poor of the world.

The rest of the Delta men set up their ambush well outside the village along the road Mohaqiq was expected to use. However, Mohaqiq must have learned that his son had died of his injuries and the warlord did not come. When they heard that Mohaqiq was apparently staying elsewhere, the team stood down outside the village to await the arrival of a helo that would bring in more ammo, MREs, and a replacement for a man killed a few days earlier. Joshua decided to stay in the village, where he could keep an eye out for any sign of Mohaqiq's intensions regarding his dead son, while helping Läkare i Världen/Médecins du Monde Sweden doctor.

A Läkare i Världen/Médecins du Monde Sweden truck, with its blue and white logo that included a dove of peace carrying an olive branch, drove through the village then stopped in a cloud of dust in front of a hospital tent where several villagers stood waiting patiently in line.

Mohamed Honsi, an Egyptian doctor, had left his lucrative practice in Al-Jizah to volunteer his services. He had only recently volunteered to work with the Swedish relief organization and had arrived in Sahr-i-Zārān from Karakalpakstan, in northwestern Uzbekistan, where he had assisted in treating more than one hundred thousand people infected with tuberculosis.

Doctor Honsi examined a boy's broken foot while his mother watched nervously through the opaque veil of her blue burka. She too was suffering from a festering wound. But because her husband had been killed during the earthquake and her uncle, her only living male relative, was fighting in the mountains, she was not permitted to be treated by this foreign doctor. If she had dared and she was reported to the Taliban, she would be shot and her son would be alone because her uncle cared only for two things—growing opium and inflicting the Taliban's interpretation of Islamic law on helpless villagers.

The Afghan driver climbed down from the cab and walked to the back of the truck where he dropped the tailgate, then flipped back the canvas cover. Joshua came out of the hospital tent to help unload medical supplies and water treatment equipment. Even though he was fluent in the more common Pashto language, and could hold his own in Nuristani, as well as Dari, the language of Afghan businessmen, he could not hide the fact that he was an outsider.

Most of the villagers, however, did not care that the young man was not one of them. They, and Doctor Honsi, believed him to be Ermanno Grossi, an Italian medical student who had taken a leave of absence from San Luigi Medical School in Turin, Italy, during his second year in order to volunteer to come to Afghanistan.

As Joshua was unloading the medical supplies from a truck and carrying them into the tent, a dust cloud appeared on the road leading into the village from lower in the valley. When he came out of the tent for more supplies, he saw the convoy of three Toyota pickups led by a black 69 Mercedes 280SE Coup. Mounted in one truck bed was an ancient 7.62 mm Degtyarev M-27 light machine gun. Another pickup carried a Hispano-Suiza HS.404 auto cannon.

He knew instantly who was coming and that he was in trouble. The Delta team had set up the ambush site in the hills because the informant had told them that the warlord would come from that direction—not from the valley. It was already too late for him to make himself scarce. He knew it would have been pointless to run because it was well known by now that he was in the village.

Women grabbed children and scurried into huts as the convoy sped through the village. Those villagers who had been waiting outside the tent melted away as the Mercedes and the pickups slid to a stop, sending a choking dust cloud over Joshua and Doctor Honsi. The tension was immediately as thick as the dust.

The back door of the Mercedes swung open and a big man stepped out. Joshua recognized him instantly. It was Abdul Mohammad Mohaqiq. Flanked by fifteen Taliban fighters, Mohaqiq watched impassively as his men closed in around Joshua as they screamed and threatened him in Baluchi, Pashai, and Pashto. He even heard a word or two in Arabic. Mostly curses and taunts, but he also heard someone say, C.I.A.

"What is the meaning of this?" Doctor Honsi challenged Mohaqiq. "We are only here to help the people."

One of the Taliban shoved Honsi roughly with an AK-74, knocking the doctor to the ground. Honsi tried to get up, but the Taliban jammed a sandaled foot into his back, pushing his face into the dust. Mohaqiq looked down in disgust at the Egyptian.

"Stay on your belly, Egyptian dog," Mohaqiq ordered in Arabic. "Or you will suffer the same fate as this CIA spy."

"He is only a boy who is here to help," Honsi protested feebly.

"He is an American. That is all I need to know about him." The War Lord motioned to Joshua, "Bring him," he ordered.

"No, wait. I didn't do anything! I am not American. I am an Italian medical student." Joshua pleaded in Pashto, as he tried to stay in character, while realizing his chances of surviving were quickly diminishing.

"You are CIA!" Mohaqiq accused, pointing a finger at Joshua. "We know this."

"CIA? This is a mistake," Joshua said, real terror starting to break his voice.

Mohaqiq turned with his hands on his hips and stared into Joshua's eyes. "We know you for what you are." He motioned to one of his men who stepped forward. "Is this the man you saw in Kabul?" he said in Pashto.

The man stepped up to Joshua and looked into his eyes with recognition. He had seen these strange eyes only once before, in a Kabul torture room. He had been an Afghan policeman then and knew the American directing the interrogations was with a C.I.A. agent and that his name was James Parris. The man nodded and smiled as he turned to Mohaqiq and answered in Pashto, "He is the same man, James Parris."

Joshua started at the name of his brother. Then he realized what was going on. They believed he was James. "Wait! I can explain. I'm not that man," Joshua tried to pull away from the grip of the Taliban killers. "I just want to—"

One of the Taliban hit Joshua in the side of the head with a rifle butt, knocking him to his knees. Two others grabbed his arms and dragged him around a building to where another man had already set up a video camera. Joshua eyed the camera. He had seen the video of Daniel Pearl's murder at the hands of Abu Musab al-Zarqawi. He knew what these men had in store for him.

The two men who held his arms pulled him across the dirt road and in front of the camera. Several others stood behind him, while two more men erected a black banner as a backdrop for their propaganda video production.

Joshua was no longer acting. He was genuinely terrified. "No, please don't do this," he pleaded.

Mohaqiq looked at the man behind the video camera, who nodded back at him that the camera was running. Mohaqiq stood directly behind Joshua, then took out a written statement that he read in Arabic, "To the war criminal Barack Obama, I show you what we do to the spies you send to my land to assassinate and commit crimes against Islam."

As Mohaqiq's voice droned on, Joshua's demeanor changed slightly. He knew he had only a few more moments to live. His mind raced. He looked up at the camera. He barely heard Mohaqiq's command, "Bind him."

The two Taliban picked him up by his arms as another man took a length of rope to tie Joshua's hands behind him. Joshua was strangely quiet, composed. The Taliban holding his right arm saw a strange expression in Joshua's eyes. He realized too late, what it meant.

Joshua struck out and hit the man on the bridge of the nose. The man felt a sickening crunch as his nose broke. Before he could react, Joshua slammed the palm of his right hand up and forced the broken cartilage into the man's brain, killing him instantly.

Then Joshua swung around, rammed his left fist in the second man's throat, and kicked the man holding the rope in the chest, sending him sprawling back toward the camera. Joshua struck again and another Taliban died. Another man raised his rifle and was about to shoot Joshua when Mohaqiq knocked it down as the man pulled the trigger. The weapon fired harmlessly into the dirt.

The Taliban guerrillas were no match for Joshua one-on-one, but they finally overpowered and drove him to his knees. He continued to struggle to rise to his feet, but he soon realized that he had run the race as far as he was going to take it.

Joshua looked up and glared in defiance at Mohaqiq as the warlord pulled a long, intricately designed, bejeweled sword—a gift from a Saudi prince—from a purple sheath, raised it above his head, and brought it down swiftly.

The man behind the camera grinned and gave thumbs up at what he saw through the viewfinder.

19

"I pray that our Heavenly Father may assuage the anguish of your bereavement, and leave you only the cherished memory of the loved and lost, and the solemn pride that must be yours, to have laid so costly a sacrifice upon the altar of Freedom." – **From Abraham Lincoln's letter to Mrs. Lydia Bixby, who lost five sons during the Civil War.**

Parris knelt in front of the headstone. He touched the engraved name and imagined he saw his brother's face in the white stone. As a twin, Parris felt that half of himself was gone forever. The better, gentler half, he knew.

Below Joshua's name were six lines that represented the totality of his existence to those of the four million who visited the national cemetery every year that might read them as they meandered among the more than three hundred thousand graves.

JOSHUA W. (Doc)
PARRIS
WYOMING
SGT. (Medic)
US Army, 75th Ranger Regiment, Company B
AFGHANISTAN
APR. 17, 1972
SEPT. 3, 2000

After the Taliban's defeat in December 2001, in response to the September 11, 2001 terrorist attack on the U.S., and the first elections took place in Afghanistan, the warlord finally surfaced from hiding. The video tape of Joshua's execution did not surface until two years later, and Parris finally knew who his brother's killer was that he now resided in Kabul, and was a cabinet minister in the new government. He would deal with Mohaqiq, but not now.

A black SUV waited at the bottom of the hill with Agent Wiler behind the wheel. He pressed an earpiece against his head and listened for a moment, then looked up at Parris kneeling at the foot of his brother's grave. Wiler didn't want to interrupt, but the clock was ticking. He got out of the car and approached Parris. "Sir, we've got to go," he said quietly.

Parris gazed intently at the grave.

"Sir, we've got to go." Wiler's voice penetrated his anger and loneliness.

"I heard you, Wiler."

Wiler was embarrassed. "Yes, sir, but they're waiting at the airstrip."

Parris took something from his pocket. He looked at the round, bronze medal with a cross and the CIA emblem, the Distinguished Intelligence Cross. He had received it four years ago for his own covert mission in Afghanistan—the one his brother had died for in his place a year later when Joshua was mistaken for him.

Other than the requisite Purple Heart, his brother received no other medal in recognition from his government for his sacrifice. His family and friends would never know that Joshua was a member of the elite Delta Force. They were not told that he was captured and beheaded. They assumed he was simply an Army medic who was just one more forgotten casualty in the *war against terror*. One of a twelve hundred or more who died in an almost ignored war compared to those who died in the more tumultuous Iraqi Freedom campaign.

Parris glanced around to make sure no one was looking then pushed the medal below the surface next to the stone and patted the ground. "They'll pay, little brother. Every one of them. I promise you."

20

Ships carrying the name Bonhomme Richard have gone to war for America since the first of the line was commanded by John Paul Jones in 1779. The second warship to bear the name was the Essex-class aircraft carrier Bonhomme Richard (CVA-31) that fought through three wars—World War II, Korea, and Vietnam.

The present ship, Bonhomme Richard (LHD-6) was the sixth Wasp-class amphibious assault ship. Homeported in San Diego, she carried eleven hundred officers and enlisted men and women, and over eighteen hundred marines. She had been deployed to the Seventh Fleet three months ago.

Now the eight hundred forty-four foot Bonhomme Richard heaved in the heavy seas like a cork, dipping down into deep troughs, then climbing up and crashing through thirty-foot, rolling waves, as it moved toward a black rainsquall. Chained to the flight deck were the ship's air complement of Marine Corps AV-8B Harrier jets, CH-53E "Super Stallion" and AH-1W "Super Cobra" helos. A Navy CH-46E "Sea Knight" helicopter approached the ship gingerly. The pilot timed his landing on the ship's pitching two-acre flight deck, as the ship dropped into another huge trough.

The wheels had barely made contact with the none-skid surface when a curtain of rain suddenly drenched the entire ship. A sailor wearing a yellow jersey shouted commands over the howling wind as several other seamen wearing blue jerseys ran toward the helo with heavy chains to "chock and chain" the Sea Knight securely to the deck. The sailors struggled beneath the helo while fighting to keep their footing or they would be blown over the side.

The back ramp came down revealing Parris and his team. Each man carried his weapons, pack, recon and communications gear, and other equipment as they headed for the ship's superstructure and went inside.

Deep within the ship, a diminutive petty officer second class, who wore a maternity shirt because she was four months into her pregnancy and was due to leave the ship when it arrived later in Yokosuka, led the team down a long passageway that rolled violently from side to side. Used to a life at sea, the young petty officer seemed to have legs made of rubber. She ambled effortlessly down the center of the deck, halfway up the right bulkhead and then the left bulkhead as the entire passageway literally rotated forty-five degrees in either direction.

She didn't bother to conceal her amusement as the team careened first off one bulkhead, then the opposite as they struggled with their heavy equipment. Sailors approaching from the opposite direction were forced to take evasive action to avoid being injured by the heavily laden commandos. The sailors hurried past the team with knowing glances. It was plain to everyone that the men were Spec Ops, but sailors on warships knew better than to ask questions, so they let the men pass without comment or nod.

It was a bruising ordeal as the men made their way through several compartments, sometimes knocking their chins on the "knee-knockers," or raised, curved metal framing of the watertight doors; and in the seemingly endless passageways, there were hundreds.

A teenage sailor, wearing a soaking wet, grease-stained apron over his dungarees, and carrying a stack of still-hot steaming metal trays with thick rubber gloves from the scullery, stepped aside as they entered one of the ship's many mess decks.

Sailors sitting and eating at the long tables ignored them. They were too busy concentrating on staying in their seats. It wasn't an easy task to hold their metal trays in place on the tables with the thumb of one hand, while with the other hand, they attempted to sip tepid soup and eat cold sandwiches. It wasn't possible for the cooks to prepare much else while under the high-seas conditions. Other sailors waited in a long line as the mess cooks ladled out soup. The sailors and marines did their best to keep their footing on the decks made slick from the broth that sloshed out of huge cauldrons each time the ship pitched back and forth.

The team filed passed the hungry sailors and clambered through the passageway on the other end of the mess deck. Then they came to an open hatch where a steep ladder led down to the deck below. The petty officer slid effortlessly down with a hand on each of the two railings rubbed slick by the thousands of hands that had made the same descent before her.

Each team member slung his weapon across his back, and then tossed his duffle bag down to the next deck. The petty officer pushed each duffle bag aside before its owner eased down the ladder carrying his weapons and op equipment, his knuckles turning white in a death grip on the handrails. Boot soles wet from the storm and treading through the soup on the mess deck threatened to take the men's feet out from under them as they came down the metal ladder. More than one of them flashed on the possibility of being injured in such an inglorious fashion and, worse, being scrubbed from the mission.

Finally, the entire team was back on a solid, if not immobile, deck, and facing yet another seemingly endless passageway. Each wondered if the journey would end soon and had the passing thought of what the hell he would do if there were an emergency and he had to find his way somehow through the labyrinth of passageways and decks back to the flight deck.

A heavy steel door suddenly swung open, barely missing the petty officer. It clang loudly against the bulkhead and started to swing back. She grabbed the steel door before it could crush one of her charges. She glanced around the edge of the door just as a young MARCO operative dressed in Spec Ops black similar to the Americans dashed passed her and across the passageway.

The operative leaped through another open door into a head, passed a row of urinals and slid on both knees until a glistening white toilet bowl was between them. He promptly wrapped his arms around the bowl and wretched what little breakfast he had been able to get down only moments before.

Wiler grinned at the marine's obvious misery, "Whooop!" he mocked, as the young man wretched again.

"Can it, Wiler," Parris said.

"Aye, aye, Boss," Wiler said and grinned as he glanced through the door, seeing the man's heaving back bent over the toilet.

The petty officer pushed down a dogging lever to hold the door in place, and then she stepped into the wardroom compartment. Three MARCOS operatives stood by Captain Vajpayee and watched silently as the Americans entered. They were drinking tea. Parris and the others recognized the red and silver winged Balidan, or sacrifice, badge on their chests and parachute regiment insignia on the maroon berets that signified the men were all members of the Para Commandos, 21st Parachute "Red Devils" Battalion.

Dark complexions, deep brown eyes, and all sporting beards and mustaches of various cuts, gave the operatives the appearance that they had been recruited from Hollywood's Central Casting for parts in a pirate movie. Not far from the truth, these men were experienced pirate hunter-killers. Each was a walking arsenal, with weapons that included 9mm Israeli UZIs and 5.56mm M16A2 rifles. Propped up in the corner of the room was a 7.62mm PSG-1/MSG-90 Sniper Rifle. Each carried his personal, curved Kurkri knife, copies of the knife originally designed for Raja Drabya Shaw, king of Gorhka, in 1727. One operative even had a lethal-looking, high-tech crossbow. The MARCOS operatives presented a dashingly dark image more akin to the cutthroats they were hunting, compared to the clean-cut, almost boyish-looking American commandos.

The petty officer closed the door behind her as she left the room. Roy smiled at the sight of Parris. "Good to see you could make it," he said. "We were beginning to worry, with this storm."

They shook hands. "Can't let a little breeze hold things up," Parris said.

The ship shuddered and the men had to grab furniture to steady them. "I'm afraid if this little breeze keeps up, we may have to postpone the mission," Roy said.

Parris motioned to his men. "We're going in, come hell or high water."

"Well, hell I am not familiar with, but I suppose you could say we're definitely in 'high water.'" Roy motioned to his men. "Sergeant Bhupad Ali," he introduced a burly, bearded, bear of a man. As he introduced the others, each nodded to the Americans, in turn. "Corporal Abdul-Baari Singh...Private Gagen Bharti, and our newest, and youngest, member, Private Rabri Pradeep Raj. Our medic."

The medic they recognized as the unfortunate sole Wiler found so amusing in his rush to the head only moments before.

Parris quickly introduced his men, who studied the Indians coolly and gave barely perceptible nods, "Staff Sergeant Dwain Marchetti...Sergeant Max Sand."

Corporal Singh eyed Sand and whispered to Ali, "The Stinger."

Sand heard the comment. He looked at Singh. The Indian seemed familiar, but Sand couldn't recall where he had seen him before. Singh provided the answer. "We met briefly at Fort Benning, at the Top Gun competition."

It took Sand a moment to place Singh. "You did good."

"A high complement coming from a renowned sniper," Singh smiled. "But not as well as you, I am afraid."

Parris continued with the introductions, "Agent Mike Jackson, Agent Gary Wiler, and Corpsman First Class Mason 'Crazy Horse' Moses."

"Crazy Horse?" Roy said curiously, remembering as a boy reading about famous cowboys and the other Indians of the American West. "You are Indian?"

Moses, a full-blooded Coeur d'Alene, and member of the Confederated Tribes of the Colville Reservation in eastern Washington State, nodded. "Long story," he said, not bothering to offer any details, which had little to do with the famous Oglala Sioux warrior, Tashunkewitko, and everything to do with a wild, nearly fatal ride through the southern Iraqi desert while behind the dual tiller controls of a stolen Russian T-72S battle tank.

"Perhaps you will share it when we have completed our mission," Roy said.

"First order of business," Parris interjected. The mood instantly changed from cordial to all business. He looked directly at Roy. "Any of your team Muslim?"

The MARCOS operatives were noticeably tense at the question. Roy was surprised at the question coming at this time, so late in the game.

"I do not see the relevance of my men's religious beliefs," he said, though he did, but hoped he might be wrong. "What if I were to ask if any of your men were Catholic?"

"It wasn't Catholics who flew into the World Trade Center," Parris said without the least attempt at demonstrating any compassion or need for political correctness.

"I stand by these men. Each has demonstrated his loyalty to our cause and to me, personally."

Parris's jaw muscles tightened and he looked at each man, then Roy. "This is not negotiable."

"You should have said something before. You cannot possibly mean to—"

"Muslims? Who?" Parris looked again at each operative.

The two lines of heavily armed men faced off, aware that they were all aboard an American warship, about to blow their joint mission over a religion co-opted by terrorists. Hands remained at their sides, away from their weapons; though each man appeared ready should someone on the other side make a sudden move. Not a muscle twitched. No one spoke.

Private Raj stepped forward. "My mother and father practice Islam," he offered. The tension in the room remained palpable. "I do not."

Parris studied the young medic. "Sunni?"

"Shia," Raj said. "I am a Christian."

"Christian?" Parris hesitated.

"Protestant, to be precise."

"That must have upset your parents."

"I would not have said it exactly that way, but, yes, they are not pleased."

Parris studied the young medic a long moment. Raj tried to meet the American's stare, but could not. He looked away. "You're out," Parris said, adding, "That's just the way it's got to be."

The other operatives started to protest. Roy held up his hand for silence and they immediately obeyed. Their eyes, however, showed their intense anger and offense at the wrong perpetrated on Private Raj. They would not forget this terrible offense.

"It is our standard operating procedure to have a medical specialist included on every mission," Roy said.

"Crazy Horse can handle any medical issues that come up," Parris said.

"It is not that simple," Roy tried to reason. "My men will only allow Corporal Raj to attend them should they be injured." He looked at Moses. "No offense, Petty Officer Moses."

Moses shrugged. "None taken, Captain."

Roy was not accustomed to discussing such things in front of enlisted men, but Parris had allowed no attempt at decorum through talking to him privately. So he was now being forced to defend his men's honor openly. "You might have communicated your concern earlier."

Parris shrugged. "Your command was adamant about not releasing personal information. Security considerations from your people stopped my people from being able to check out each of your men's backgrounds. We weren't given your team's roster until your bird was in the air. It looks like some bureaucrat made the decision that we did not have a need to know."

Roy looked at his other men, then at Private Raj. "I intend to register an official complaint."

"Do what you've got to do, Captain. But be aware that we, too, have our share of bureaucrats. No telling what will happen to it. Meanwhile, we've got a job to do. Is your team in or out?"

Roy stiffened, made a sharp about face to Private Raj, who came to attention. Not much older than some of the teenagers who served aboard the Bonhomme Richard, Raj was incapable of masking his disappointment as he saluted his commanding officer. He turned and left the wardroom without a word. His comrades were dismayed. There was a long, uncomfortable moment as the two alien groups eyed one another suspiciously.

"Have some tea, lads," Roy said to the men.

Outwardly, the men seemed to relax as they helped themselves to tea, coffee, and pastries. But harm had been done to the unity of the Special Forces team that needed to be established in order to better its chances to for success.

Roy took out a piece of paper and smoothed it on the table. "Members of Abu Sayyaf engineered a prison escape of fifty-three militants."

"I thought the Abu Sayyaf was pretty much wiped out two years ago," Sand asked, looking at Parris for confirmation.

"Green Berets and Filipino troops managed to reduce their numbers from several thousand to a couple of hundred," Parris said.

"Their leader, Khadaffy Janjalani, is being financed by Jemaah Islamiyah in Southeast Asia," Roy said. "We know that most of them are based either on Basilan or Mindanao, but they have begun to infiltrate even Luzon, much to the embarrassment of President Arroyo."

"Well, let's see if we can help Mrs. Arroyo by eliminating some of these bastards," Parris said as he took a chart from his rucksack and spread it on the table. "By steaming all night, we should be within range of Mindanao about the same time as the eye of this storm."

"That would be a break," Roy said.

"A lucky one, if it happens," Parris said. "We'll be coming from over the horizon, so our window is limited. The back end of this storm may catch up with us before we hit landfall. It's going to be close." He looked up from the map. "Needless to say, we must not be detected by either the Abu Sayyaf or Philippine troops. Once we find their camp, we secure any available Intel, then grab the nuclear material and get the hell out of there."

"What about prisoners?" Bharti asked.

"What prisoners?" Parris said.

Bharti was puzzled that the American did not apparently understand the basic question. "What if some of them surrender or are wounded?"

Parris took a long moment before answering. "We do not wound the enemy, so there will be no problem with prisoners," he said. "Understood?

The Americans looked at one another. This was a new kind of fighting for most of them, but they all acknowledged with nods that they understood Agent Parris's meaning. Bharti was new to the MARCOS team and had not been involved in its previous engagements against the fanatical Muslims. The other MARCOS operatives, though, were accustomed to the terrorists' determination to kill as many of the infidels as possible before their ultimate death at their enemy's hands or at their own. The operatives didn't have a problem with the order. They would have been surprised if there was a requirement to take prisoners. Bharti looked from his comrades to Parris, and then at Roy for confirmation. "I understand, Agent Parris."

"Comments? Questions?" Parris said to both teams.

"We have been fighting these people for many years," Roy said, holding out his hand to Parris. "We welcome America to *finally* join us." He leaned close to Parris and whispered, "You are in command only because my government has acquiesced to America, again. But I will not tolerate continued maltreatment of my men, as I am sure you would not allow such of your men."

Parris looked up at the taller man a long moment. He knew that he had not handled the situation as he should have, but he was incapable of admitting fault. He also knew he needed Roy's unquestioned cooperation, if not his loyalty. Parris was not here to make friends. He was here to carry out his mission, and he would work with whomever it took to accomplish it. He nodded to Roy and they shook hands.

Parris glanced at his watch. "It's going to be a rough fifteen hours before we get in range for takeoff. Everyone get some rest. Have your gear ready in the hanger bay by zero four hundred."

21

Because of the nature of its mission and the need to control rumors, the team was isolated in one of the smaller berthing spaces. The space was self-contained with its own head, and was comprised of modular bunk beds. Each bunk had its own curtain that provided meager privacy, and a small reading lamp mounted in the upper corner. The bunks were designed so that the bed was the lid to the locker where the fifteen sailors who normally slept here stored their clothing and personal items. It was often said that many prisons afforded their inmates more personal room than sailors had aboard most ships.

It was a few minutes after one in the morning, when Moses woke up. He lay in the bunk a few seconds as he tried to remember where he was. The room was dark except for a red light near the floor. He could hear men snoring and the sound of creaking metal as the ship swayed.

In an effort to smooth the MARCOS operatives' ruffled feathers a bit, he had drunk several cups of tea as they got to know one another better. Now he really needed to piss. He had put it off because of the ship's constant rolling and pitching. There was no putting it off any longer. He didn't look forward to trying to make it to the head, but there was no choice, his swollen bladder couldn't take the beating from the ship's incessant pounding any longer.

Moses released the strap across his chest that held him firmly in the bunk and swung out, careful not to bump his head on the bunk a little more than a foot above his own. He inched out of the bunk, stood and held onto bunks on either side of the narrow row between them for balance. He was careful to hold on to a bunk on either side to maintain his footing.

A single red bulb lit the head. Moses held onto a pipe that ran across the bulkhead above the six urinals. Water sloshed out of all six and spread across the deck to a drain.

Barefooted, he tiptoed around the streams of water and straddled one of the urinals. It proved to be a difficult maneuver as he tried to hold himself with one hand so he could avoid urinating on the deck as he grasped at the pipe in front of him with his other hand to keep balance as the ship suddenly pitched violently upward.

Moses managed to finish without pissing on his feet and turned to a row of stainless steel sinks to his left. Just as he stepped toward the sink nearest him, the ship took an unexpected roll, and he lost his balance. He stepped into one of the streams of water pouring out of the urinals and his feet started to slip out from under him.

"Oh, shit!" was all he could manage while fighting to keep from falling. But the entire room suddenly shifted nearly forty-five degrees and he was slammed violently against a sink, striking his right elbow. He instinctively grabbed it with his left hand as the pain shot up through his arm. Instantly, he knew he was in trouble and his worst fears came to pass as he was hurled across the room, crashing into a metal stall. The loud snap of his shoulder breaking was the last thing he heard before he passed out.

22

Later, Parris, Roy, Raj, and Marchetti watched as two corpsmen carried Moses, now conscious, out of the head on a stretcher. The ship's doctor, a lieutenant commander, followed and turned to Parris, "His collar bone is shattered," he said. "It's a clean break. We can set it in sickbay. He's going to be laid up too long to do you any good."

"Thanks, commander," Parris said. "I'll come up later to see how he's doing."

"We should be finished in about an hour."

"Yes, sir." Parris placed a reassuring hand on Moses' chest. "Take it easy."

"Sorry, sir," Moses said in a blur of pain. "I screwed up."

"Hey, things happen," Parris said. "You've got to admit it, though, even for Crazy Horse, this is pretty good."

Moses groaned as much from the pain as embarrassment at his own absurd predicament.

"But I don't think I can write you up for a medal this time."

Moses grinned at Parris. "No purple heart, huh."

"I'll see you up in sickbay. The doc is going to take care of you."

"But you're going to need a corpsman?"

Parris nodded to the two sailors at either end of the stretcher. They picked Moses up. Parris looked at Roy, then back at Moses. "Don't worry about it."

The corpsmen moved down the passageway. Parris turned back to Roy, and then glanced at Private Raj. "All right, Private, you're in. Get your gear ready."

The boy grinned broadly, "Yes, Sir. You won't regret it, Sir," he said, then ran as fast as the pitching ship allowed him down the passageway.

"I hope not," Parris murmured.

"You won't," Roy said. "He's a good soldier—and an excellent medic."

"We'll see." James murmured, just clearly enough for them to hear.

23

By four o'clock in the morning the typhoon had subsided somewhat, but the wind was still blowing across the deck at more than seventy miles per hour, category one level. Only on a ship the size of the Bonhomme Richard would a seaman consider the waves tolerable. Sailors checked the chains that secured the thirty helicopters and eight Harrier II aircraft.

Their Ch-46 medium assault helicopter was warmed up and the teams hurried across the deck to climb aboard. Carrying only their weapons and backpacks this time, the going was much easier than it had the day before going down into the ship and they made their way up the ramp to the helo.

"The storm picked up speed during the night," Parris shouted over the noise to Roy. "Our window is down to half an hour."

"We won't make it to the LZ in time," Roy shouted back. He gave Parris a knowing look as they walked up the ramp into the helo. The others strapped themselves in for the bumpy ride ahead.

Parris handed Roy a piece of paper. On it were a set of GPS coordinates. "Our inside man will leave info there on where the camp is," he said. "They move around between several camps every day or so, so he won't know the present location until the last minute."

Roy showed a *thumbs-up* sign that he understood.

The navy helo pilot received the all clear signal from the yellow-shirted aircraft handling officer and pulled back on the stick as the craft lifted off and banked left over the frothy sea. They were now flying at one hundred sixty miles per hour in the eye of the storm and the sky above was a brilliant blue, but dark thunderheads loomed just a few miles in every direction around the helo. The helo immediately dropped out of sight as it skimmed only a few feet above the crashing waves and raced toward an, as yet, unseen island over the horizon in an attempt to beat the storm.

They didn't make it.

24

The commandos held on to keep from being injured as the helo jerked violently, pitched, and shuddered as the storm threatened to rip it apart and toss their torn bodies down into the cold, grey, water, that was being churned into a frothy white foam by the howling wind. The pilot and co-pilot fought to keep the machine flying against the typhoon winds that now raged at category two levels of between ninety-six and one hundred ten miles per hour.

They managed to keep the helo flying just above the surface of the water. Then the leading edge of a huge wave swooped up and struck the aircraft broadside, nearly engulfing and pulling it down into the water. The engine sputtered and threatened to die all together. It took sheer brute power on the part of both pilots as they each pulled back on the stick with both hands and the two GE-T58-16 engines—along with God's merciful hands as far as some aboard felt—to convince the machine to regain altitude above the waves. Not bad for an aircraft designed by the Boeing Vertol Company to serve Marine Corps combat and evacuation missions in Vietnam over forty years ago.

The men exchanged concerned looks. Private Bharti inflated his life vest. Jackson grinned at Bharti and shouted, "Won't do you any good, if we have to ditch." He rapped with his knuckled on the metal beside his head. "These things are top heavy. They flip over in the water. Not likely anyone would get out."

Private Bharti grinned sickly. "Thank you. So good of you to let me know."

"You bet. Better to know what's real, and what ain't, I always say." Jackson grinned broadly. "No sense getting your hopes up."

"I appreciate the thought." Bharti pulled the life vest tighter around his chest, anyway.

The pilots continued their struggle to control the eighteen-thousand pound aircraft. They peered through the windshield and the curtain of water. Finally, they spotted the outline of the island ahead of them. The pilot called back to the team over the radio, "Three minutes to LZ."

Parris pressed the headpiece to his lips and shouted back to the pilot, "Roger." He made a circling motion with his hand to the team. "Three minutes."

No one had to be told what to do as they began securing their weapons and equipment, attaching everything tightly to themselves. Wiler and Marchetti managed to get a heavy rope out of a locker and tied one end to a brace overhead. The pilot fought the controls to steady the helo as it flew a few feet above a jungle canopy. "One minute," he spoke into the microphone. He heard Parris respond through the headset.

Parris and Roy stood on either side of the round "hell hole" hatch in the center of the floor and looked down at the jungle. The trees pitched wildly and sheets of rain drenched everything. They looked at each other across the open hatch. It was time.

"Beautiful day for dropping in on friends," Roy shouted across the hell hole.

Parris grinned, and then turned to the men. "Ten seconds," he called out. He looked again down to the trees as the helo flared. He kicked out the heavy rope and watched as it tumbled down through the high branches, then disappeared in the thick foliage.

Parris and Roy helped each man as he made his way to the hatch. Marchetti grabbed the heavy rope with his gloved hands, glanced down, then winked at Parris just as he dropped through the hole. In a moment, he had disappeared into the greenness below. Singh, Ali, Jackson, and then Raj followed Marchetti's example without incident.

Sand stepped up to the hellhole and grabbed onto the rope. "See you guys down below," he called out, then dropped toward the jungle canopy below. But a heartbeat after he dropped through the hatch, the helo suddenly lost altitude, and then just as rapidly jerked back up. Sand was yanked roughly up and down like a yo-yo. He tried to fast rope down through the trees, but the helo was out of control, dragging him behind it. Sand's body flipped up and down like a rubber toy soldier being dangled from a string as it was being pulled through tall weeds. He crashed through tree trunks four or five feet thick in a wild, dangerous and potentially deadly ride. Sand kicked himself clear of one huge tamarind tree, and then crashed headlong through the branches of several cedars.

Parris shouted to the pilots and grabbed a hatchet from its bracket, placed there specifically for this purpose and braced himself to cut the rope in an effort to save Sand and possibly the helo, "Get this damn thing under control or you're going to kill him!"

"Get him off there or we're going down," the pilot radioed back frantically.

Parris and Roy exchanged quick worried looks; Parris spoke into his microphone, "Max, look for a soft spot."

Knowing exactly what Parris was about to do if he didn't do something himself, Sand looked frantically for a landing spot, preferably, if possible, one without any protruding rocks or trees. All he could see was a carpet of green foliage below him. Then he spotted a small clearing. He let go of the rope and plummeted through the trees, telling himself he knew this was going to hurt like hell.

With Sand's two hundred thirty-five pounds suddenly gone, the helo rapidly regained altitude. As Parris and Roy watched wide-eyed, Sand's body fell to earth like a cannon ball shredding tissue paper as he slammed through the trees and bamboo.

At first, Sand thought he would make it without any major damage. Then he collided with a thick branch that knocked the wind out of his lungs. His forward momentum caused him to flip forward, and the heavy pack and equipment on his back carried him over. He didn't have much time to think about it. Every branch felt like a sledgehammer, and the biggest jolt of all was when he finally hit the ground. He had thought he'd be dead—there was no way he should have survived what could best be described as an uncontrolled descent. It was beyond control. But he was, remarkably, alive, though not totally unscathed.

If not for the heavy rain that had turned the clearing into a bog, Sand guessed he would have died from the fall. As it was, he found himself nearly buried in thick, red mud. Now all he had to worry about, he reasoned through the fog of being mugged by the trees, was to keep from drowning in the ooze.

He struggled to get his hands under him and pushed up with all his strength. Luckily, there was a degree of solid terra firma a few inches below the layer of mud or there would have been no hope of freeing himself and possibly sinking out of sight. He could hear the sucking sound and felt like the mud was an alien force intent on holding him in its embrace until he weakened, and then gorging itself on his limp body. The equipment on his back threatened to hold him down as his eyes peered above the muck. However, he was a man of tremendous strength and he finally managed to get his face clear and take a much-appreciated lung full of wet, dense air.

In the helo, Parris could see Sand spread eagled in the wallow. At first, he thought Sand must be dead, but then he saw him struggle up to his feet. As Sand stood up, the mud and water dripped off his battered and bruised body like clumps of wet clay. He looked up to see a water buffalo standing at the edge of the wallow, slowly chewing on a mouth full of wet grass. The buffalo didn't seem the least bit concerned as it lowered its head to crop off another wad of grass. Sand nodded at the buffalo. "Don't mind me, big fellow. Just thought I'd drop by, but I got to be going now."

The pilots were finally able to level off over the trees and called back to Parris and Roy, "Now's as good as a time as you'll ever get, gents. Good luck."

Parris motioned to the hellhole, "After you."

"If you insist," Roy said, as he bowed slightly, grabbed the rope, and dropped swiftly through the trees to the high grass.

The others watched from below as Roy, and then Parris, fast-roped down to the jungle floor. As Parris hit the ground, the helo turned sharply and immediately disappeared in the downpour.

The men gathered around Parris as he took out a miniature GPS locator. He studied it a moment, and then motioned to his right. As they moved through the rain forest canopy and thick undergrowth that did little to abate the downpour, Parris kept a close eye on the locator while the others kept watch as best as they could through the soul-drenching rain for any sign of their prey.

Parris checked the locator against the coordinates on a plastic-coated topographical map. "Look sharp. Our contact indicated she would leave directions to the rebel's camp at these coordinates," Parris said.

They spread out and began searching. A few minutes later, Private Raj called out, "I think I found it" He pulled on a small metal tube nailed to a tree. He took the tube to Parris, who opened it and took a piece of small, yellowed cigarette paper. He opened it carefully and saw a crude, hand-drawn map with the coordinates of the secret rebel camp. He handed it to Roy, who asked, "How far?"

"No more than two hours, I figure," he said and put the GPS locator back in his pocket. "That way," he motioned. They turned south and headed deeper into the forest.

Two hours later, after drudging through miles of thick forest and wading countless swollen streams, the team waited as Private Bharti crawled on his belly ahead of the others. He looked down from a bluff into a wide grassy clearing where he saw several huts. Through the rain, he could see smoke rising from the tops of two of them. He turned and looked back over his shoulder and waved for the others to move forward. Parris and Roy crawled up next to Bharti, who pointed down toward the huts. Parris studied them through his binoculars. It appeared that no one in the village was eager to venture out into the rain. "No security?" Parris whispered, curious.

"Not very smart of them," Roy said. "It is a wonder they have eluded government forces for as long as they have."

"They probably have scouts out that would spot army patrols." Parris said as he continued to study the camp. He motioned for the men to take positions around the camp. As they moved away, he took out a small motion sensor, activated it, stuck it into the ground, and then switched on the miniature monitor attached to his vest.

The men spread out until they formed a wide circle around the camp. Each set a motion sensor in place and began moving in toward the camp. The rain was their ally. It kept the terrorists inside the huts and it covered any sound the commandos may have made moving through the mud as they crept closer to the camp.

Sand, Wiler, Singh, and Ali approached from the tree line to the west. The two snipers, Sand and Singh got into position and covered Wiler and Ali as they moved in and spread out. To the north, Jackson, Bharti, and Raj made their way through the grass. Parris and Roy kept low as they ran across open ground to the east of the camp, leaving Marchetti and Raj to cover the southern trail entering the camp. There were five thatched huts surrounded by rivers of slick red mud. A five hundred pound feral hog waddled between two of the huts, nudging its snout through piles of garbage. The rain beat the smoke coming from the huts back down until it settled around the camp like a London fog.

As Wiler edged around a huge pile of rubble and trash, he nearly stumbled over a boy of about twelve-years-old who was just buttoning his pants after relieving himself. Wiler brought up his weapon and the boy jumped back, his eyes filled with terror. His mouth opened to cry out, but the scream choked in his throat. He stared at the American commando and started shaking. He looked just like what he was, a wet, emaciated, terrified child.

Wiler pointed his weapon at the boy's face. The boy dropped to his knees and started crying and begging in Tagalog, as he covered his head with his hands. Wiler looked around and saw Ali disappear behind a hut to his right. He knew the snipers could not see him or the boy because the trash pile obscured them from view. He looked back down at the cowering boy and nudged him with his toe. The boy looked up through tear-filled eyes. Wiler glanced again toward Ali, who was too far away to see what he was doing. He motioned with a nod toward the forest. The boy looked at him with a puzzled expression. Wiler lowered his weapon and motioned again toward the tree line.

"Get out of here," he whispered desperately. "Go. Now."

The boy got to his feet slowly and bowed to Wiler, as if to thank him, then started to trot toward the forest. Wiler watched him for a moment, and then brought his weapon up and turned to approach the nearest hut.

"American." Wiler heard the child's voice calling to him. He looked over his left shoulder and saw the boy smiling a child's smile at him. What is that kid doing? He has to get out of here. Wiler thought. Then he saw the round, green metal object the boy tossed underhanded toward him.

Even though his training told him what the object was, he could not stop himself. It didn't matter that his mind was screaming for him to jump for cover because his left was reaching out instinctively to snatch the object as it arched slowly toward his face. He caught the object like a popped up foul bal, looked at it, and he knew in that instant that he had just made the dumbest mistake of his life—and his last. Wiler saw the boy grinning like a mischievous child who had just pulled a harmless prank on an unsuspecting adult. Then the boy waved bye-bye to Wiler as the M67 fragmentation grenade exploded.

The boy turned and started to run into the forest. His back exploded in a crimson splash of blood and bone from the impact of a heavy bullet. His small body was hurled forward and sprawled face down in the mud. The wild hog's massive hairy head rose up from rooting nearby and eyed the lifeless form with interest.

Jackson lowered his silencer-equipped weapon. He closed his eyes a moment at what he had just done and at what had just happened to his friend. He didn't want to, but he looked down at the smoking remains of Wiler's body. For just an instant, his eyes showed the sadness and loss of a close friend, but in a second, the look was replaced with one of determined rage.

At the same instant as the explosion, Roy was standing in front of one of the huts. Upon hearing the explosion, he raised his right leg and kicked in the dilapidated corrugated iron door. His brown eyes swept the dimly lit, smoke-filled room. He saw four people—three men and a woman. The men had most likely heard the muffled explosion, but with the rain beating incessantly on the huts, it had not registered as something to be overly concerned about. They were still squatting around an open cooking fire as the smoke drifted up to a hole in the thatched roof. One of the men was just ladling a handful of sticky rice and bits of fish with a bent spoon from a rusty cast iron kettle. Another was hungrily sucking on a silvery fish head. The third was fingering the rice on his cracked porcelain plate.

In that moment, Roy also saw the woman's dead eyes staring at him. Her bloody hands were bound with barbed wire, pulled over her head, and tied to a rattan bench. Her shirt and pants had been ripped away. Her legs were broken and spread-eagled. Her breasts were lacerated and the lower half of her body was covered with her own dried, putrefied blood. He knew she must be their *inside man.*

Apparently, the terrorists had figured it out too, but she must not have talked even after such horrendous torture because the commandos had not been intercepted on their way to the village. She had been dead for some time, yet the men ate undisturbed by her presence. They looked up when the door burst from its leather hinges. All three were dead before they could stand.

Bursting through the wall of another hut, a seven-foot-tall Japanese giant tried to escape. The man had long pomaded hair that clung to his massive head as he ran. He was covered from neck to ankles in brilliant red and blue tattoos depicting dragons and geishas. He wore only dingy pair of green boxer shorts with dancing reindeer from someone's distant Christmas past. Six much smaller men kept close behind the tattooed giant leaping across the clearing for the protective forest, trying desperately to get away from the killing zone.

At the tree line, Sand and Singh sat a few feet apart, their arms resting on their knees as they waited. They had heard the muffled explosion, but could not see what had happened. Now they could see some of the terrorists heading in their direction. They each straightened. Using his riflescopes, Sand tracked with the tattooed giant, sighting on the man's head. The man was so big it would be impossible to miss him—even on the run. Still, Sand glanced at Singh to see how he was taking in the strange sight. The nearly naked Japanese giant was running for his life in a Philippine jungle, leading a gaggle of diminutive Filipino Abu Sayyaf terrorists. *Terrorism breeds strange bedfellows,* Sand thought.

Singh zeroed in just below the chin of the smaller Filipino running behind the giant. As the seven men slogged through the mud across the clearing, Sand and Singh each took a single shot. The giant toppled like a felled tree and the smaller Filipino dropped like a bag of wet cement.

Suddenly leaderless, the remaining five scattered. Sand followed one man and as he scrambled over a large rock, Sand's bullet threw him to the ground when it hit the man in the sternum.

Singh centered his sight on another man's head just as the man turned to raise his weapon. The man's head exploded. Whether it was instinctive or if the men had decided their only hope was to stand their ground and fight, the three remaining terrorists turned back and opened up on Sand and Singh with their AK-74s on full automatic.

Sand jumped behind a long dead acacia tree for cover a split second before it was shredded by a full burst from one of the AK-74s. One round tore Singh's rifle from his hands and the shattered weapon dropped to the ground. In a swift, fluid move, Singh slipped off his crossbow, with an arrow already in place, and fired from the hip. The small, black arrow with its hardened steel tip streaked across the clearing in a blur and pierced one of the terrorist's throats.

Sand had moved to Singh's left and got off a single shot. It blew out the kneecap of another of the three. The man screamed in agony and fell to the ground.

Singh notched another arrow just as the last man was taking aim at Sand. The man was just squeezing off the shot when the arrow hit him just below the second rib on his left side, piercing his heart. Before he dropped, the man managed to get off a single burst and Sand dropped to his knees and rolled over on his side.

In one of the huts, two terrorist commanders desperately attempted to burn a pile of papers. The pouring rain and dampness of everything made it difficult to keep the flames going. One man tore at a codebook and threw the tattered pages into the smoldering pile, then waved his hands to fan the flames. He turned at the sound of a foot kicking against the door. With a second kick, it burst open. Parris stepped through the splintered door with his weapon raised. "Who's going to tell me where the nuclear materials are?" he said without preamble, pointing the SAW M249 light machine gun at them so there would be no mistaking his intent.

The shorter of the two men said to his comrade in Tagalog, "Say nothing."

Parris shot the man with a three-round burst in the chest. "Bad advice."

Blood from the dead man's still pumping heart spurted on the other man's face and arm, and then the body crumpled to the dirt floor. The other man looked down in stunned silence, then back at the American. He raised his hands. "I talk, you no shoot?"

"Depends on what you've got to say," Parris lied.

Singh knelt beside Sand and rolled him over. Sand groaned softly and Singh pushed aside Sand's right arm and saw where two bullets had hit the American just above the belt. No organs had been hit, but blood soaked the lower part of his shirt and right half of his pants. Sand opened his eyes and he looked at Singh, "Help me up, would you, pal." He gritted his teeth as Singh helped him to his feet.

"Here, you may need this," Singh said and handed the fallen sniper rifle to Sand.

"Thanks." Sand gratefully took the rifle in his left hand and leaned on Singh's arm for support.

They looked toward the huts at the sound of firing. "After you, my friend," Singh said, motioning with a nod of his head toward the camp.

"You bet." Sand forced himself through the pain to move as he clutched the rifle to his chest with both hands. They had only taken a few steps when they heard moaning coming from the bushes. One of the wounded terrorists was still trying to crawl away, his blood trailing after him. The man's lower leg dragged, hanging from the shattered remains of his right patella by a single fleshy muscle as he desperately tried to escape into the refuge of forest. Singh took his intricately decorated Kurkri knife and stepped away from Sand.

"You don't have to do it, Singh," Sand said. "He'll bleed out before he gets to the trees."

"Perhaps. But now we'll be sure of that."

Sand knew Singh was right.

The badly injured man heard Singh's footsteps behind him. He glanced fearfully over his right shoulder and saw Singh. Then he saw a glint of light in Singh's hand. The man whimpered and struggled to crawl faster, still thinking he could make it to the trees. Then he looked back again, and this time his body stopped and his eyes widened as Singh walked almost casually toward him, the Kurkri in his hand. When the desperate terrorist tried to move, his ripped leg snagged on a rock. He cried in pain and pulled forward with both arms and the bottom of his leg broke free. He dragged himself hand over hand, leaving behind him an ever-widening trail of blood.

A horrendous scream from somewhere outside the hut jolted the remaining terrorist commander. He had started talking about the nuclear materials, James's SAW still aimed at his chest, but now he was silent. He didn't know which one of his men had just died at the hands of these infidels, but envisioning a razor-sharp blade slicing through his own throat, he knew his chances of living beyond the next few moments were in fact zero. He knew his fate and accepted it. And he was determined to take this one with him.

With a groan and looking suddenly sick, he reached under his shirt and pulled a Russian IZH-70 Makarov pistol from his waistband. The weapon had not cleared his pants as a fist-sized hole exploded in his chest and his intestines erupted from his stomach. There was no time for even a glimmer of a last thought as he was ripped apart by the fusillade from more than one weapon. Parris turned and saw Roy standing in the doorway.

25

Later, Jackson, Bharti, and Marchetti searched the circumference of the village for bodies, dragging them into the huts out of sight. Bharti pointed to a blinking motion sensor monitor attached to Jackson's Kevlar vest. "Isn't that supposed to make a noise, too?" He said, already knowing the answer and wishing he were wrong.

Jackson looked down at the monitor as it blinked at him. He tapped the miniature device with his index finger and it started chirping. "Oh, shit," he said as the others realized the audio alarm on the device had failed. The team stopped instantly, realizing instantly their situation. They could hear the sound of several people, who they knew must be more terrorists, approaching only seconds away. There was not time to set up an ambush.

The commandos turned to face the forest just as two columns of heavily armed men and women stepped into the clearing. Having had the deep Jolo forest to themselves for the decade without being detected or hunted down by government forces, the Abu Sayyaf had carelessly meandered back to their camp with their weapons still slung carelessly over their backs. They had also neglected to send anyone out to cover point.

The two groups of heavily armed men stared at the other in surprise.

The carnage was instantaneous. With weapons on full automatic, the commandos laid down a solid wall of fire that cut into the Abu Sayyaf's ranks. It was a terrible field of slaughter as the bullets shredded bodies, ripping chunks of flesh away, exposing the inner flesh of chests, and bellies. Faces were torn in apart. Scalps were ripped away with the tops of skulls.

But even as they were butchered alive, the terrorists managed to return sporadic fire, eight of the men and women in the column nearest to the camp were killed and another five were crippled, but not before Jackson was hit several times in his legs and face. Finally, a shotgun blast eviscerated him from his throat to his belt buckle.

Bharti and Marchetti saw Jackson fall, but had to stand their ground, legs spread wide apart for support, weapons held firm at their hips as they fired into the moving mass of soft flesh, bone, gristle, and raw fanaticism that made up the Abu Sayyaf force as they continued to fight rather than run.

Hearing the battle as it began, Raj had sprinted between the huts, fearing for his friends. Parris and Roy ran out of the hut, saw their men's desperate situation, and sprinted through the clearing to join the fight. Upon hearing the first shots, Singh was still helping Sand on their way to join the others. By the time they got to the fight, it had already transformed.

The commandos' 21st century high-tech gadgetry and sophisticated weaponry were instantaneously rendered useless as fifteen surviving terrorists surged forward in the deathly embrace of ancient warriors, fighting hand-to-hand.

Machetes, bolos, Kurkri, and Bowie knives slashed and stabbed. The eyes of an Abu Sayyaf fighter bulged in terror as Bharti strangled him. A woman ran a long, rusty bolo through Ali's arm only to lose her own head from Bharti's Kurkri. Another man shot Raj in the back, but his Kevlar vest saved him. Roy killed that man instantly.

Parris and Roy fought shoulder-to-shoulder as the Abu Sayyaf threatened to swarm over them like deadly army ants eager to consume a hapless insect that had stumbled into their midst. A rifle butt hit Parris in the side of the head and a blinding flash tore through his consciousness. He fought on, enraged and bewildered, as he slashed out blindly with his combat knife. Someone struck a powerful blow to his lower spine, driving him to his knees. Unable to rise on his own, he thought he must surely be mortally wounded, but Roy pulled him up from behind and Parris fought on through the horrifying haze. His mind was a whirling blur of red gashes, greens, browns, and blacks, and the smells of the slaughter nearly overwhelmed him.

Parris smelled the unmistakable aroma of cordite. Curiously, the smell brought back flashes of week long hunting trips for elk with his father, his uncle, Earl, and his brother, Joshua. They would hike into the higher elevations in search of the elusively shy animals and like many life-long hunters, the trip was more of an excuse to leave the world of work and the thousand other tasks that took up every waking moment. He had never thought of the smell of cordite. Now he could come up with a smell to compare it. It was simply one of those smells that triggered a memory.

Parris knew that from now on the smell would mean something different to him. The smoky cordite that hung thick over the blood soaked ground of this jungle would mingle not just with unpleasant memories of escapes from reality, but also with the other odors of innumerable battlegrounds. Unwashed bodies, stagnating, weed-choked mud soaking up the combatant's blood. Rancid bile, along with putrid fecal and burning urine smells all blended as men lost control of their bowels, the effect of white hot metal and sharp blades ripping their bodies apart, spilling their intestines over the ground to mingle with the ripe fragrance of pungent wood smoke as the village burned to the ground.

26

Parris sat on a rock swaying gently back and forth, as he looked down at his boots. He thought idly there was no way he would be able to clean the mud, slick scarlet blood, and gore from them. Hell, he'd have to throw them away, and he'd just gotten them broken in. He struggled to remember where he was and what had just taken place and why his back was killing him. Oh, yes, someone had rammed him, probably a rifle butt against his lower spine. Now he remembered. He was down. A tangle of struggling bodies hovered all around him as he tried to regain his feet. Someone reached down in all the chaos and pulled him up. Who? Did it matter? No. He was alive. That's all that mattered.

"James, are you all right?" Roy's voice penetrated the fog. It was the first time Roy had called him by his first name. Their relationship had changed. They were no longer individual warriors from different nations. They were comrades-in-arms who had fought and killed a common enemy together. Parris looked up and his eyes were red with blood from the blow to his head. He tried to focus. "We've got to be going." Roy said. "The helo is on the way."

Parris stood and looked around the camp. The dead lay all around them. Gun smoke, rain, and fog that clung to the still warm bodies gave the scene an eerie, netherworld look. Apart from the enemy dead lay the bodies of Special Agents Wiler and Jackson, and Private Bharti. Sand was badly wounded but functioning and Ali's right arm hung in a bloody makeshift sling. The others, with torn uniforms and covered in blood, went about the business of piling up the enemy dead and preparing for liftoff when the helo eventually arrived.

"Come with me. You need to see something," Roy said as he led Parris between the huts to where Sand and Singh had killed the seven men who had tried to escape into the forest. Parris followed Roy along a game trail. He stopped and motioned to one of the bodies. Parris pushed aside the grass and knelt beside the dead giant, studying the prone body.

"Nice work," Parris said of the tattoos.

"Those are irezumi tattoos.'

"I've heard of those."

"He had to be a member of a Yakuza gang. They're the Japanese mafia. A rather nasty breed of mobster," Roy explained.

"You sure?" Parris looked at Roy, glad *he* was thinking clearly.

"Look at his left hand."

Parris rolled the body over to pull the man's left arm from under him. The first joint of the little finger was missing.

"It's called 'yubizume,'" Roy said. "The Yakuza demand absolute loyalty. If any member commits even a minor transgression, they must amputate the last joint of the little finger and gift-wrap it as a present to the oyabun, or father figure. Yakuza consider it a badge of honor and openly display it in order to intimidate shopkeepers and restaurateurs to get preferential treatment."

Parris stood as he continued to study the body, more out of curiosity and amazement. "So, what's a Japanese gangster doing hanging out in the middle of the Jolo rain forest with the Abu Sayyaf?" he asked rhetorically.

"He is possibly also a member of the Red Brigade," Roy offered. "With this fellow's presence, we have reason to suspect a connection between Abu Sayyaf and the Yakuza, and perhaps even the Red Brigade."

"We heard the Red Brigade disbanded after Fusako Shigenobu was arrested." Parris rubbed his aching head. That was in Osaka, wasn't it? Back in 2000?"

Roy nodded. "We have intelligence from North Korea that there are possibly others still operating. Hijacking ships and blowing them up is something the Red Brigade would be involved with if the opportunity presented itself," Roy said.

Parris looked at the body again. "I'll have Marchetti take some pictures of our friend here and we'll pass them along. We better get the hell out of here."

"With all these connections, surely someone must have sent for reinforcements," Roy said.

They made their way back through the huts and stepped over and around the twisted and grotesque remains of the dead. Roy glanced to his right at the sound of a 9mm Beretta as Marchetti dispatched one of the survivors. Distracted, Roy stubbed the toe of his boot and looked down at what had tripped him up. It was a moldy briefcase, still gripped firmly in a dead terrorist's hand. Roy started to pull the briefcase from the man's fingers and he was caught by surprise when the man's eyes opened. Roy stared mesmerized as the man pointed a snub-nosed Smith & Wesson 360 revolver at him and he started to pull the trigger. The man's head snapped to the side as a heavy blood-covered boot connected with his jaw.

Roy looked up and smiled in relief at Parris. They both looked around at the devastation and death all around them. *How would this first joint mission be appraised?* They had made costly mistakes and been vastly outnumbered. The two teams had worked well together. Their weapons were superior, which gave them an edge until the Abu Sayyaf overwhelmed them and resorted to hand combat. Why had they prevailed? Ultimately, the outcome was determined by superior training and a dogged determination to survive—a lethal combination as it turned out.

27

"The size of a commercial vessel can make it a 'soft target' simply by the fact that the crew complement cannot maintain an adequate watch while underway. Most vessel operators are concerned with what lies ahead, not with what lies astern. Except for the occasional check of the radar for any overtaking ship traffic, very little time is spent keeping a watch astern. This creates a perfect situation for the maritime criminal who desires to board a vessel while underway. By using small high speed craft, they enjoy a measurable success of boarding large deep draft commercial traffic by approaching from the stern." – **Maritime Security.com bulletin**

In the tradition of her eight sister ships that were named after Australasia birds, the Northwest Swan was North West Shelf Venture's newest LNG ship. Built by Daewoo Shipbuilding and Marine Engineering in South Korea, she set out on her maiden voyage in April 2004, from the owner's LNG loading facilities at Withnell Bay in Western Australia.

Longer than three football fields, at more than nine hundred forty-one feet, and with a draft of almost thirty-eight feet, it could take the ship nearly five miles to come to a complete emergency stop.

Operated by ChevronTexaco Australia, the ship regularly made the run between Western Australia and Japan, passing between East Timor and the sixty-six islands that made up the Tanimbars. Then the ship transited the Philippines by way of the Malacca Sea, Celebes, Sulu, and then South and East China Seas, as she made her way to any one of the Japan's twenty-three LNG terminals.

On this trip, she was bound for the Sodegaura terminal with more than thirty-six million gallons of super cold liquefied natural gas in order to top off the thirty-five storage tanks belonging to Tokyo Electric.

Using a membrane containment system, the Northwest Swan, painted black and red, with huge white LNG lettering on her sides, looked more like a conventional freighter rather than her older sisters with their four insulated, glistening white spherical tanks that resembled four snow cones, which marked them for what they were—floating bombs.

Highly automated, the Northwest Swan carried a crew of less than two dozen. And, as predicted by the Maritime Security bulletin, her crew was incapable of protecting either the ship or themselves.

As the ship now lay dead in the water, swaying gently in rolling seas fifty-eight miles off East Timor, most of the crew was gone—having already been weighted down with machine parts and scrap metal, and then jettisoned overboard alive like so much trash. Only those who could help maneuver and power the giant ship had been spared by the fifteen heavily armed men and women that made up the collective of terrorists comprised of Abu Sayyaf, Aceh, and Jemaah Islamiah. All were in league with Al-Qa'ida, and they had followed the ship in powerful speedboats and overtaken her just before sunrise a day out of port.

The ship's captain and second in command were herded up to the bridge. The engineering crew was taken below to get the ship moving again. Demolition experts, members of the terror group, secured explosives to the outer sections of the storage tanks, along with secondary incendiary devices, crucial to their plan. Two senior terrorist officers made their way deep into the ship with their 'special' package.

28

The seven surviving Special Forces commandos sat silently as the Sea King helo approached the Bonhomme Richard. An eighth man sat shivering, manacled and gagged between Sand and Marchetti. Each of the Americans was over six feet tall and each was a product of many hours in the gym weight room. They towered over the diminutive figure between them. Either would have happily strangled the little man and tossed him out the open side door into the sea, as they looked sullenly at the black polyethylene bags lying on the helo deck at their feet containing the bodies of Wiler, Jackson, and Bharti.

Parris had sidestepped his own 'take no prisoners' order when he had hauled the still unconscious man from the ground and tossed his limp form into the helo as it touched down in the camp. One glimpse at the contents inside the briefcase and he knew that the little man clinging to it was a crucial link to the missing nuclear materials, which he now knew were no longer on Jolo.

The helo touched down on the flight deck and the back ramp began to lower. Ali and Singh picked up Bharti's body. Though wounded, Sand helped Parris carry out Wiley. Marchetti and Roy took Jackson. They carried the bodies down the ramp solemnly. In the full light of day, they looked like they had just stepped out of hell itself. Their black uniforms were covered in blood and they reeked of death. They stared ahead with eyes dead of emotion.

The sailors on the flight deck nearest the helo stood in awe and shock as the Special Forces commandos marched across the flight deck carrying the body bags between them. Most of the sailors aboard the Bonhomme Richard knew they would never have to see firsthand the terrible toll of warfare on human flesh. While some stopped to ogle the commandos, many of the sailors kept to their normal routines, either oblivious to their presence or too embarrassed at not knowing how they should react.

But not Isaac Cobb. The six-foot four, two hundred sixty pound former starting right tackle for the Minnesota Vikings, who was currently serving as the Master Gunnery Sergeant of the ship's marine detachment of eighteen hundred marines from the 2nd Battalion, 3rd Marine Regiment, III Marine Expeditionary Force, happened to be crossing the flight deck.

As a Marine who had seen men fight and die up close and personal in Vietnam, Iraq, and Afghanistan, Isaac Cobb interpreted the sailors' nonchalance as a lack of respect of major proportions. The veins in his tree-trunk thick neck bulged and his chest tightened with barely controlled rage as he bellowed: "Attention on deck! You will show some respect!"

Even though Master Gunnery Sergeant Cobb was not in their chain of command, the sailors knew instantly that they had fucked up big time. They knew that the battle-hardened Marine was right in calling their disrespect to their attention in no uncertain terms and that they had not reacted appropriately to the commandos, particularly the dead.

Every man and woman on the flight deck came to attention and turned to face the procession. As the commandos passed Cobb, he snapped to rigid attention and saluted the men. Parris looked the Master Gunnery Sergeant in the eye, and a silent recognition between warriors passed between them.

29

Later, while Ali and Sand were being tended to in the ship's sickbay, the rest of the team sat sullenly around a long table in a small room filled with high-tech gear, computers, and LED screens. Parris paced as Roy and the others watched stone faced. On one of the screens, Secretary Stone's eyes seemed to follow Parris as he paced "What do you mean the materials have been disbursed, Agent Parris?" Stone quizzed.

Parris looked in the direction of the screen where he knew a miniature camera attached to its side was broadcasting his image back to Homeland Security in Washington. "That's what I said, Mr. Secretary. I have no reason to believe those documents are misleading. The Abu Sayyaf weren't expecting us to get our hands on them. According to the documents, in addition to the materials that were used against the Bali Song Flower, the materials were divided up between three more cells."

"My God," Stone said. "Any idea what these other cells are targeting?"

"No, sir. Not at the moment."

"What about the prisoner? Do you think he has any information?"

"If he has anything, we'll get it out of him, sir." Parris said as he glanced at Roy.

"The clock is ticking, Agent Parris. We need that information ASAP."

Parris looked at his watch. "I'll get back to you, sir."

"Sooner than later," Stone said. He picked up a document and studied it a moment. He looked back up and added, "There is a JAG lawyer aboard the ship who is attached to the UN mission. I thought you should be aware of that."

The screen went blank. Parris and Roy exchanged a look. "A UN barrister?" Roy said. "That could complicate matters. Human rights and all, you know."

"I'll talk to this lawyer and tell him how things are going to be," Parris said. He looked to each man. "Get some rest. I'll be down later."

30

The UN lawyer, a Navy lieutenant, turned out to be a stunning redhead who had been around the legal block a time or two. Scrubbed clean of the gore and blood, and wearing crisp, non-descript uniforms, Parris and Roy showed no outward evidence of their recent mission and their surprise as they joined the ship's executive officer, Commander Taylor Jessup, in helping themselves to coffee and sat down in comfortable chairs.

With a slight French accent, Lieutenant Jeanette Devereaux sat across from them and looked unflinchingly at them. "Since the incidents at Abu Ghraib and Camp Delta, no prisoner will be interrogated without council present, Agent Parris. Is that clear?"

Parris glanced at the executive officer. "I understand where you're coming from, Lieutenant, but we don't have time for this."

"I'm sorry if due process is an inconvenience," she said. "But I can't permit an unauthorized interrogation, particularly since the prisoner is injured and needs to remain under medical care."

Parris held his temper. He knew the officer was only doing her job, but he felt that her *due process* would inevitably result in untold numbers of death and amounts of destruction. "This little son of a bitch is injured because he tried to kill Captain Vajpayee. We know he was behind the hijacking of a ship and the murder of its entire crew, along with several thousand tourists aboard a cruise liner."

This was news to the Bonhomme Richard's executive officer. "Are you telling us you believe this man was responsible for the Bali Song Flower incident?"

"I wouldn't exactly call it an *incident*, sir." Parris was barely able to hold his contempt for the word. "He arranged the murder of over three thousand innocent people."

"Allegedly," the JAG lieutenant interjected as she turned to the executive officer. "Commander, I strongly recommend you keep the suspect securely confined until proper authorities can arrive—"

"Lieutenant," the executive officer interrupted as he leaned forward in his chair to face the lieutenant head on. "I *am* the proper authority aboard this ship." He turned back to Parris. "You can talk to the prisoner, Agent Parris. But you are to handle the situation professionally and within the dictates of international law."

"I wouldn't think of doing otherwise, commander," Parris said coolly.

The JAG lieutenant was clearly disturbed at the turn of events. "Sir, I wish to register my highest objections to Agent Parris conducting this interrogation of the suspect," she protested. She eyed Parris as she made her intensions clear to him, "If the suspect should be harmed, you will be subject to criminal charges."

"I'll keep that in mind," Parris said. He rose to leave and nodded to the executive officer. "By your leave, Commander." Parris and Roy stood to leave. "I'd appreciate it if you'd let the master-at-arms know we're on our way down to the brig." He offered his hand to the executive officer, who shook it firmly.

"No problem. He'll be expecting you."

31

Parris and Roy walked briskly down the passageway. "How do you plan on getting him to talk to us?" Roy asked.

"I'll take the direct approach," Parris said cryptically.

Roy gave him a quizzical look as Parris knocked on the door to the brig. A burly sailor opened a bard window and looked out.

"You Agent Parris?" the Chief Master-at-Arms asked, even though he knew very well who Parris was. The word had spread throughout the ship about the Special Forces team and its take-no-bullshit leader. The Chief Master-at-Arms glanced at Roy.

"My assistant," Parris said.

The Chief Master-at-Arms gave Parris a knowing look and opened the door. The cell door clanged open. Parris and Roy stepped in and their captive turned to face them. The side of his head was bandaged where Parris had kicked him. The Chief Master-at-Arms started to close the cell door behind them. "Other than telling us his name, he hasn't said a word since you brought him down here," he said.

"Okay, Chief. Thanks." Parris said and turned to the prisoner.

There was a small window in the door for observing prisoners. Roy eased to his left to stand in front of it and leaned against the door to block the curious from looking in or listening.

"You mind sharing your name with us?" Parris said.

"Carlos," said the Abu-Sayyaf terrorist. "I am a prisoner of war. I demand to see a lawyer. I will only tell you my name, rank, and—"

"I don't have time for this shit," Parris said, and then he hit Carlos in the chest with a straight-armed karate blow, knocking the smaller man over a chair and into the opposite wall.

Parris looked back at Roy to see if there was a problem with his direct approach. Roy looked concerned, but he didn't object.

Parris reached down, grabbed Carlos by his shirt collar, and hauled him to his feet. "I want to know which cells have the nuclear materials and their targets." He jammed Carlos down into the chair. "And I want to know it now."

Carlos smiled. "You are not very clever. You think you can use force to make me talk? Fortunately, America is a nation of laws. This is illegal and anything I may say will not be admissible in court."

"Clever?" Roy said. He looked at Parris. "I would never accuse Agent Parris of being clever." He winked at Parris.

"And who said anything about you appearing in court?" Parris said. "We know what you are. We know that in most cases you would never give us any information that might harm or stop your Muslim brothers from killing innocent people."

Carlos folded his arms across his chest. "I do not have anything to say to the two of you."

Roy and Parris exchanged a look. "We'll see about that," Parris said.

32

Parris dragged the protesting Carlos into the ship's massive well deck. Marine mechanics turned at the sight of the Special Forces commando hauling the Filipino terrorist between three huge LCACs, or Landing Craft, Air Cushioned, in Navy speak.

Master Gunnery Sergeant Cobb stepped up to them. He looked at the young marines under his charge, then at Parris. "Is there something going on here that my marines shouldn't be witnesses to, Agent Parris?" Cobb said in the way of men who know they are doing unconventional—and even possible illegal in a conventional world.

"You got a rope, Master Gunnery Sergeant?" Parris asked crisply.

Master Gunnery Sergeant Cobb turned to a marine private. "Private, get Agent Parris, here, a length of line."

The private jumped at Cobb's soft-spoken command, "Yes, Master Gunnery Sergeant."

Carlos looked pleadingly at the marine through tear-stained eyes. "Please, help me," he begged. "He will kill me, if you don't."

Cobb looked at the terrorist a moment, then at Parris. He knew the score and didn't want any of his young marines to be involved, even if peripherally. He shouted over his shoulder to the men, "Marines, muster in the berthing compartment for weapons' inspection. On the double!"

The private trotted up with a length of rope. "Here's the line, Master Gunnery Sergeant," he said. Cobb took the line and motioned with a nod for the private to move out. The young marine took off without a backward glance. As young and curious as he was, he knew instinctively he didn't want to be in the well deck with these men when the shit hit the fan.

Cobb waited until all of the marines were out of earshot and turned to Parris. "You know we've got UN people aboard."

"Better join your troops, Top" Parris said, using the more casual term for a Master Gunnery Sergeant.

Cobb glanced at some of the marines who were taking their time leaving the well deck, wanting to see whatever action was about to take place. "Move it out, marines," he bellowed, as he turned to leave.

"Top," Parris stopped him.

"Yeah?"

"On your way out, hit the ramp button, will you?" Parris asked.

"Sure thing," Cobb said as he turned smartly and left them.

Parris nudged Carlos toward Roy, who held the trembling man by the shoulders. Parris began to make a loop in the rope. Then he placed it around Carlos' neck.

"What are you doing?" Carlos said, his voice trembled uncontrollably.

"Trolling," Parris said as he took up the slack in the rope.

Carlos was confused. Then there was the blaring of a klaxon, followed by the rumble of the big ramp at the back of the well deck as it began to descend. Parris hauled Carlos by the rope toward the ramp as it continued to drop.

It suddenly dawned on Carlos what was in store for him when the ocean appeared, a swirling, bubbling cauldron behind the moving ship. He pulled back in terror. "No," he cried out.

Parris yanked on the rope. Carlos stumbled forward. He was terrified and tried to pull away as they reached the edge of the ramp that hung out over the water. Parris seemed to be contemplating the open ocean for a moment. He turned around and looked at Roy.

"It's a magnificent day to be alive, isn't it," he said theatrically.

"Yes, it is, indeed" Roy agreed, not sure just how far Parris would go with his wild scheme, but pretty sure the American would go as far as it took to get what he wanted out of Carlos.

Parris looked at Carlos with a slight smile. "Ready?"

Carlos wasn't sure what he was supposed to say. All he could muster was, "What?"

Parris punched Carlos in the nose, which immediately began flowing crimson red down the front of his face and splashed on the dungaree shirt he had been given when he was put in the brig. Parris leaned down, examined the results of his work with satisfaction, and winked at Roy, as he also examined the bloody work.

"I think that is sufficient," Roy critiqued.

Carlos held his nose and looked back and forth between his two tormentors, pleading with his tear-filled eyes. He looked out at the water fearfully. "I will drown and you will get no information," he said defiantly.

As frightened as he was, Carlos was a fanatic and his back stiffened in resolve. Even though he was determined to keep these men from extracting information from him, there were the beginnings of stark terror creeping up and eroding that resolve. But, for the moment, he resisted and jutted out his jaw defiantly. "In the name of Allah, I—"

Parris grabbed him by the scruff of the neck with his left hand and the belt with his right and heaved Carlos out over the ramp and into the sea. Carlos screamed. Then he disappeared into the froth and bubbles. The rope panned out like fishing line from a reel and just as the end was about to fly out into the water, Parris stepped on it.

A few seconds later, Carlos popped up about thirty feet behind the ship. He clung to the rope desperately with both hands to keep from being dragged by his neck like a baited hook trolling for a big marlin. His body bounced in and out of the water. He choked and coughed up water and his submerged again, twisted underwater and came to the surface again. He flipped over on his back and was able to keep his head above water for a moment, but was again pulled under. He looked like he was caught in a gigantic washing machine, tumbling end-over-end in endless bubbles. He gagged and breathed in salt water. Blue sky. White bubbles. Fathomless darkness below. Then something dark skittered passed him. Parris and Roy watched as Carlos' body flipped out of the water like a playful porpoise and disappeared again in the froth.

High in a catwalk surrounding the well deck behind them, two sailors, a third class petty officer and a seaman apprentice, stepped out of an open door for a smoke and looked down at the LCACs. As the seaman apprentice flipped a silver Zippo to light the other's cigarette, he looked toward the back at the open ramp curiously. He snapped the lighter shut, squinted, and motioned for his friend to look.

"What the fuck?" the seaman apprentice said.

"Hey!" the petty officer shouted down to the two men standing on the ramp. The very tall, dark one turned and looked up at him.

"What the hell's going on?" the seaman apprentice said.

"Jesus, look at that," the petty officer said, pointing at the two men as one of them grabbed a smaller man by the back of the neck with one hand and his belt with the other.

The seaman apprentice looked to where his friend was pointing just as the little man was tossed out over the waves and just as quickly disappeared. "They're drowning the little fucker," he said as he stubbed out his cigarette. "We've got to tell someone."

"Who?"

"How the fuck do I know!" The seaman apprentice grabbed his friend by the arm and yanked him back inside the ship.

In the well deck, Roy turned back to Parris after seeing the two sailors leave. "We're running out of time," he said. He looked back through the well deck and didn't see anyone yet.

Carlos' screams were growing weaker. He could barely hang on to the rope and he was submerged more often than not. From his vantage point, when he did manage to pop to the surface, he could see his two tormentors standing on the ramp. Then he was pulled under the water. He could no longer hold his breath and gagged as the salt water rushed into his nose and mouth. He knew he was going to drown.

Then he saw the dark shape again. An instant later, a grey sleek form raced below him and as he surfaced again, he saw the shark's sharp dorsal fin slice through the water between himself and the ship. *It was one thing to give one's life for Allah; it was quite another to be eaten alive.* He flipped over on his back and screamed one last desperate plea, "Shark! Please, help me!"

Roy shifted nervously. He was beginning to think that perhaps they had stretched the little man's luck too far. Then he saw the shark's dorsal fin and the long tail. There had to be fifteen feet between the two fins. He nudged Parris and motioned to the black shape slowly creeping up behind Carlos.

"You do want him to talk to us, don't you?"

Parris had seen the shark too and started pulling hand-over-hand on the rope, but not too fast. "Just one little bite?" He played Roy's nerves.

But Roy was ready. "I'm afraid one bite from that monster might also consume the information we still very much need to retrieve from our diminutive friend."

The shark suddenly disappeared. Then they saw the dorsal fin coming up fast behind Carlos, and they knew it was time to get their game out of the pool. Roy grabbed the rope and together they reeled in Carlos, as the shark closed the gap.

Roy pulled faster. "We do need him to talk."

Parris gave him a quizzical glance and picked up the pace, but it looked like the shark just might take a nibble out of Carlos before they could get him aboard. They gave one heave and Carlos flopped on the ramp like a blue fin tuna as the shark swirled nearby, then turned on its side, eyeing them with its huge yellow eye, and dove beneath the surface.

Laying face down, Carlos heaved up seawater and tried to suck in air simultaneously. It was working very well. Parris nudged Carlos with the toe of his boot and rolled him over onto his back. Carlos's eyes rolled back as water gurgled out of his gaping mouth. Parris pushed on the terrorist's stomach with the palm of his hand and watched him wretch painfully, expelling the last seawater. He grabbed Carlos by the belt and hauled him to his feet.

"There, all better?" Parris said sounding sincere, but not in the least so.

"Have we got your attention?" Roy asked, as he and Parris held the soggy terrorist up, his legs too wobbly to sustain himself.

"Master-at-arms, put Agent Parris and Captain Vajpayee under arrest!"

They turned in unison as the JAG lieutenant approached them, in tow with the Chief Master-at-Arms, several of four of the burliest sailors aboard the ship, along with a very unhappy looking Commander Jessup. For her part, however, Lieutenant Devereaux looked extremely pleased with herself at having nabbed the two in the act of breaking God only knew how many UN provisions, not to mention UCMJ laws.

"We were just getting his attention, Lieutenant Devereaux," Parris said.

"Let go of that man, right now," she ordered.

Parris and Roy exchanged a glance, then obliged her and released Carlos, who promptly crumpled to the deck in a puddle of water that had been gathering at his feet. She glared at them and Parris shrugged back at her.

"Commander," she demanded.

Commander Jessup turned to the Chief Master-at-Arms. "Chief, take them into custody."

"Yes, sir," The Chief Master-at-Arms said, and nodded to his men, as they flanked Parris and Roy. Parris motioned to Carlos and said to one of the sailors, "Watch him for me, will you son," he said, as he looked down at Carlos. "This isn't over."

"Take them to the brig," Lieutenant Devereaux ordered the master-at-arms detail.

Commander Jessup stepped forward. "If you don't mind, Lieutenant."

Lieutenant Devereaux realized she had overstepped herself. "Yes, sir. I didn't mean to—"

The executive officer ignored her. "Chief, you can take them below."

The Chief Master-at-Arms turned to the executive officer. "Yes, Sir." He then motioned for Parris and Roy to come with him and his men. "Agent Parris, Captain Vajpayee, this way, please."

As they led Parris and Roy away, and as the sailor started to take Carlos by the arm, Parris called back to him, "This isn't over, Carlos."

33

A tall marine in full dress uniform stood next to the door of the ship's commanding officer's stateroom. He snapped to attention and opened the door as Commander Jessup approached. Jessup removed his hat as he entered the stateroom.

Captain Charles Bauchman was a thirty-five year mustang, or an enlisted who was promoted to the officer ranks. He had first seen sea duty as an aviation ordinanceman on the flight deck of the aircraft carrier, USS Oriskany (CVA-34), after leaving home at seventeen to escape the dreary existence in a Pennsylvania factory town.

Jessup approached his desk. He had had been Captain Bauchman's friend for more than twenty years and served as his exec for the last three, so he knew something was wrong before Bauchman said a word.

"Skipper?" Jessup stood in front of the mahogany desk, hat in hand.

Bauchman glared and didn't invite Jessup to sit down as he normally would have. "Exec, I think you must know that I don't like getting my ass chewed out one damn bit." He fingered a stack of papers in front of him.

"Sir?"

Over the years, the two career sailors had had more than their share of good times—this was not going to be one of them. Jessup could not remember the last time Bauchman's face was as red as it now was or when the blue vein in his forehead pulsed as it now did.

"I don't like getting my assed chewed on by the Secretary of Homeland Security. And I really don't like getting my ass chewed out by the Chief of Naval Operations." Bachman grumbled.

"The CNO, sir?"

Jessup began to sweat and the heavily starched khakis scratched at his thick neck as he wished he was anywhere but standing in front of his friend, whom he realized he had somehow let down. It was an exec's job to protect his commanding officer from being blindsided, and he had apparently failed miserably.

"And I absolutely don't like getting my ass reamed by the President of the United States."

Jessup deflated into the chair in front of Bachman's desk. "The President, too, sir?"

Bauchman's eyes narrowed. "You *have* heard of the Patriot Act, haven't you, Commander." Jessup realized he had taken the liberty of sitting without being given permission to do so. He stood back up and came to attention.

"Yes, sir, I have. Though I haven't read it. I'm pretty sure where this is going."

"You have no idea." Bauchman shook his head as if to shake away his anger. He nodded for his friend to take the chair. "This Agent Parris seems to have friends in very high places." He pushed a priority message toward Jessup, who picked it up as Bauchman leaned back in his leather chair. "We've been told he's strictly hands off. He wants something; you make sure he gets it. Understood?"

Jessup looked up from reading the terse message with a return address to the Chief of Naval Operations. "Crystal clear, skipper."

"This is no way to run a Navy, and I don't like it one damn bit. But that's the way it is." He looked at Jessup as he bit on his lower lip nervously. "I want everything documented to keep this from coming back and biting me in the ass. Homeland Security and the President may have the upper hand right now in using the Patriot Act to bludgeon anyone who gets in their way, but if Congress has anything to say about it, especially since the President signed on to McCain's torture ban, we may all end up spending our retirement years at Leavenworth Prison." He drummed his fingers on the highly polished desk. "I'd have to agree that what Agent Parris did to this Bagsic fellow was damn well beyond what the good senator from Arizona had in mind for cruel and unusual treatment of detainees."

Jessup took a deep breath and ran his fingers through his thinning hair. "What about the JAG officer, Lieutenant Devereaux?" he said, hesitantly, hating to even acknowledge that she could be a major speed bump in keeping things low key, if not totally under wrap.

"What about her?" Bauchman was embarrassed at his momentary lapse at having forgotten to take into consideration the young officer who, in his opinion, appeared to have more allegiance to UN than the America and the U.S. Navy, both of which she had sworn an oath to defend. This was a serious shortcoming for a naval officer, as far as he was concerned. "Oh, yes, I see what you mean."

Bauchman thought a moment as he continued to drum a cadence on the desk. Then he looked up at the Jessup. "Being that we are now *officially* under the scrutiny of Homeland Security, it would be prudent for JAG to examine each crewmember's personnel jacket. And don't forget the marine detachment. If we have any security risks aboard, I want to know about it sooner than later."

"That's more than two thousand people, skipper?"

"Yes, I'm aware of that." He smiled and poured himself a cup of dark black coffee from a stainless steel carafe. "Have Admin deliver the records to her stateroom, ASAP."

Jessup got up to leave. "I'll see to it, sir." He started for the door.

"And Jessup..."

Now what, Jessup thought as he turned back. "Yes, sir?"

"I don't want JAG out of her quarters until we pull back into San Diego."

"Three months, Skipper?"

"Have her meals taken to her."

"Can we do that?" Jessup was clearly uncomfortable with the idea of what might amount to false imprisonment of Lieutenant Devereaux. He thought it highly likely that she would interpret it that way. "She's JAG, Skipper. She'll know you can't do that without charges."

"Read up on the Patriot Act. I'm sure you'll find something applicable in there to keep her out of the loop until this resolves itself," he said, even though he knew that it was highly unlikely and thought, *I'm going to end up in prison, and what the hell for?*

Jessup couldn't help from arching his eyebrows in amazement. "You absolutely sure about this, Skipper?"

Bauchman's eyes narrowed. "You want me to pass the next call from the CNO or the President to you?"

"I'll get right on it, sir."

"Good. Dismissed."

Jessup stepped outside the stateroom and eased the door shut. He leaned against the bulkhead for support and took several deep breaths to compose himself. The marine corporal looked at him. "You all right, XO?" he asked.

Jessup pushed away from the bulkhead, looked at the young marine. "Yes, Corporal."

"You sure, sir? You don't look—"

"Carry on, Corporal."

"Yes, sir," the corporal stiffened and thought the executive officer was a real asshole as he stared straight ahead at the bulkhead across from him.

34

Parris swung the cell door open. Carlos was seated at the steel table resting his head on his arms. He looked up as his tormentor entered the room and jumped up, knocking the chair over. He backed up against the bulkhead.

"Carlos, you look disappointed to see me. You hurt my feelings."

"To hell with your feelings," Carlos spat. "I tell you nothing."

"So you said before," Parris said as he closed the cell door behind him. "We'll see about that."

35

Parris and Roy worked in the small stateroom. Parris studied a laptop linked to Homeland Security. He was talking to Stone, while Roy pecked away at another laptop, checking an Interpol database.

"Do you think he's telling the truth?" Stone asked.

"Yes."

"Got it," Roy said.

Parris looked at Roy's screen. "Link us up," he said.

Roy punched a couple buttons. "Done."

The image on Parris's screen split. Stone was on the left side and the Interpol record on the right. It showed the personnel records of a Filipino merchant seaman, Edward Bagsic, Carlos' brother.

"You see this, Mr. Secretary?" Parris spoke into the microphone attached to the laptop.

"Yes. He's serving as a deckhand on a ship named Northwest Swan."

Roy typed away and his screen flashed different Web sites that he was not sharing yet with Parris and Stone, until he came to one for the shipping company that owned the Northwest Swan." As Roy typed a flashing, red warning indicator appeared on screen. He tapped on the link and read the message.

"James, you better take a look at this," Roy said.

Parris leaned over and read the seafarer's alert. "This is bad."

"What is it? Stone asked.

"The Northwest Swan is an LNG ship. She pulled out of Withnell Bay a week ago bound for Japan. She hasn't been heard from for the past three days." An image of ship appeared on

Roy's screen. He brought up the ship's vital statistics page. "She's carrying nearly thirty million gallons of liquefied natural gas," he said and looked at Parris.

"I'll have someone contact the owners. Let's hope the ship is equipped with tracking equipment," Stone said.

"She was built only last year, Mr. Secretary," Roy said. "She should be so equipped."

"They could have disabled it," Parris said.

"That would throw a wrench in the works," Roy said as he returned to searching the Interpol Web site. "Wait." He read the Interpol page on the computer. "It just got worse," he said.

"What did he say?" Stone said.

"He said it just got worse," Parris said, looking at Roy for a hint of what he meant.

"How could it get worse than having a bunch of terrorists with a nuclear device on a ship filled with liquefied natural gas?" Stone demanded in frustration.

"It would appear there are four Bagsic brothers," Roy said.

"Four?" Parris said and looked at the Interpol page.

Roy read the Interpol information to them, "All four are members of Abu Sayyaf. Carlos, who we already have in custody, is the eldest. Edward, as we now know is on the Northwest Swan. The other two are—"

"You're serious?" Stone said, already knowing the answer.

Parris speed-reads the document. "Interpol has nothing on the other two other than they are also merchant seamen. But they can't find any record yet whether they've signed on with any vessel," he said.

"Yes," Roy said excitedly. "Another brother, Fernando, is a wiper aboard the Hanjin Sur, which belongs to a Japanese and Qatar consortium. She's headed for Osaka, and is due to arrive in two days." He looked over at Parris, who knew immediately by his expression what was coming next.

"It's also an LNG vessel," Parris said as he turned to face the screen to tell Stone.

"Get your team to Manila," Stone said. "I want you in Osaka to stop this Fernando. Send me the details on the fourth brother and I'll see if we can run him to ground."

"Mr. Secretary?" Parris said. "We're going to need reinforcements."

"Get whoever you need."

"What about the Northwest Swan? She's most likely headed for the closest major port city." He brought up a map of Australia on the screen. "My guess is Sydney. If that's the case, we should—"

"I'll get back to you when I find out something. For the time being, we have to go for the target we know."

"Yes, sir. But if it should turn out to be Sydney, they have to evacuate."

Stone didn't blink. "Let's hope it isn't." He started to turn away, and then turned back to the monitor. "Parris. Captain Vajpayee."

"Yes, sir?" Parris said.

"Yes, Mr. Secretary," Roy added.

"I'm sorry about your men. They were brave soldiers and their sacrifices will not go unforgotten."

"Thank you, Mr. Secretary," they both said. Nevertheless, it did not make them feel any better about the loss of three good men.

36

The Northwest Swan cut through the waters of the South Pacific fifteen miles off the Australian coast. Edward Bagsic leaned on a railing on the right bridge wing and watched the lights of Brisbane slip by. He looked at the silver Rolex Oyster Professional Sea-Dweller 4000, newly acquired from one of the ship's officers, who no longer needed it as his body hovered in several fathoms of the Arafura Sea. It was 3:15 A.M.

Right on schedule.

Someone inside the bridge dialed in a Brisbane radio station. The radio personality's voice drifted out through the open door: "This is New Day Australia, and I'm John Kerr, with you from midnight to five, every weekday on Brisbane's News Talk 4BC, 1116 on your AM dial. I'll be talking with Stuart Woods about his newest *Holly Barker* novel. Then I will play again my recent interview with Ringo Starr, who will be celebrating his birthday bash with the family in Sydney next weekend."

Fernando shut out the banter as he thought about his brothers and their mission. It had finally happened. The world would not soon forget the Bagsic brothers or the cause of the more than fifteen thousand strong Abu Sayyaf organization. They had survived three attempts to assassinate them: two by Philippine Army that failed, and then one by a traitor, who struck while the brothers were visiting their parents in Cebu. The traitor, along with a hired killer, machine-gunned the parent's modest home one evening during dinner. They succeeded in killing the brother's mother and sister, and badly crippling their father.

Unfortunately, for the killers, the four brothers had gone out that night and were at the local *Cinema One*, where they were enthralled watching their childhood movie star hero, Fernando Poe, in the last film, before his death, *Pakners*.

It had taken the better part of a year for the brothers to hunt down the traitor, but they finally caught him when he foolishly returned to his family home in Tagaytay, in the mountains of Cavite Province. While Fernando held a wire garrote around the traitor's neck, he forced the man to his knees to watch as his three brothers systematically slaughtered the man's parents, a brother, two sisters, a brother-in-law, and twin six-year-old nieces. After they were all dead, Fernando pulled the man's head back so he could look into his eyes as strangled him, very slowly.

While they had eliminated one enemy, they had made many new ones in the province because besides being a member of Abu Sayyaf, the traitor was also a high-ranking, popular police officer. They had not been careful in covering their tracks when they came to town and soon not only was the AFP, Armed Forces of the Philippines, after them, but the local and national police forces were also actively searching for them.

And the police officer's remaining family set a bounty of five hundred U.S. dollars for each of their heads, instantly propelling them into folk hero status. Before the assassination of the policeman and his family, the Bagsic Brothers were small-time criminals and minor players among the Abu Sayyaf. After the murder, some may have admired them as the depression era poor of America vicariously followed the exploits of the likes of Dillinger or Bonnie and Clyde , but many among the Filipino poor were more pragmatic. Five hundred dollars was two years salary in Cavite Province.

The bounty on the Bagsic Brothers made it necessary for them to return to the deep forests where they were relatively safe among their fellow terrorists. From there, they mounted their attacks on tourists, missionaries, and passing ships. It was a fortunate night when they happened on the slow-moving British freighter and its secret cargo. Now, Edward was returning

a portion of that cargo to the infidel, as would his brothers, Fernando and Jessie.

37

Inside the Bonhomme Richard helo on its approach to Japan's Atsugi Naval Air Facility, where an Air Force C-141B Starlifter waited, Parris listened to the distant voice of Tom Rhodin, Deputy Commissioner of the Australian Federal Police (AFP), "I don't know if I can do that, Agent Parris." Rhodin had only taken over the deputy commissioner's duties a week earlier. The former office holder had been cheering along with eighty thousand other cricket fans for the home team as it struggled to overpower the visiting South Africans when he died of a massive heart attack.

Now Parris had to convince the new deputy commissioner that despite the suspect nature of Carlos's information, the Intel was serious and urgent. Parris spoke into the mike, "You really don't have a choice," he said bluntly. "The ship was hijacked by members of Abu Sayyaf—"

"The Philippine group?" Rodin asked skeptically, and then unable to accept what he was hearing, "Sydney? Why Sydney, for Chris 'sake?"

"Listen to me!" Parris barely managed to control his anger and frustration. "We have intelligence that Sydney is their next target."

"Next? What are you saying?"

Parris took a deep breath to calm his own voice. "We now know that members of the Abu Sayyaf managed to get their hands on nuclear materials. They then coordinated with a Somalian terrorist organization to use a portion of those materials when they destroyed the cruise liner, Bali Song Flower. Because the ship was at sea, the casualties were limited to the three thousand aboard the liner. The entire area of the explosion is now contaminated" He paused a moment to allow Rodin to absorb the information, then added, "The Northwest Swan is carrying millions of gallons of liquefied natural gas and has the potential to obliterate your city, sir. Over four million of your people are at risk."

There was a pause on the line. "Please hold," Rhodin said. The line sounded dead, the nature of the secure connection to allow no interference, but Parris knew Rhodin was conferring with his own advisors. Then Rhodin was back. "It is our understanding that it is nearly impossible to ignite liquefied natural gas because of its extremely low temperature," Rodin said

"That's up for debate. Do you really want to take a chance that you're wrong?"

There was another long pause. "How reliable is this intelligence?"

Parris looked at his watch and closed his eyes a moment. "Can you see the harbor from your office?"

"Yes,"

"Look out your window," Parris said. "The Northwest Swan should be visible now, sir."

A moment later, the Australian's voice came back over the radio, "It's just turning into the Western Channel off Quarantine Head," Rhodin said, then added crisply, "Good-bye, Agent Parris."

The line went dead and Parris turned to Roy.

"God help them," Roy said.

38

"An ignited LNG vapor cloud is very dangerous because of its tremendous radiant heat output. Furthermore, as a vapor cloud continues to burn, the flame could burn back toward the evaporating pool of spilled liquid, ultimately burning the quickly evaporating natural gas immediately above the pool, giving the appearance of a `burning pool' or `pool fire.' An ignited vapor cloud or a large LNG pool fire can cause extensive damage to life and property."
California Energy Commission, July 2003.

Darling Harbor, originally called Cockle Bay because of the abundance of shellfish, is Sydney's industrial hub with docks, a rail yard, and an international shipping terminal. It is close to Chinatown's famous Garden of Friendship, designed by Guangdong Province landscape architects.

The harbor is also home to the vast Sydney Convention and Exhibition Centre, over two dozen hotels and apartment buildings that feature some of the most innovative modern architecture in the world, particularly at Cockle Bay Wharf and King Street Wharf. Overlooking the harbor is the port city's most prominent architectural feature, the Sydney Opera House, with its six gleaming spherical roofs designed by Danish architect, Jorn Utzon. Nearby, is Sydney Harbor Bridge, built in 1932. Once nicknamed the "coat hanger," locals now simply referred to it as "the bridge." With eight lanes, it is the main artery between North Sydney and the City of Sydney. Its two landfalls rested on The Rocks to the south. The opposite end rested in Kirribilli, an exclusive neighborhood that is home to Kirribilli House, the residence of Australia's prime minister, as well as the Admiralty House, where the governor-general of Australia stayed when in Sydney. Both men would normally be staying far away at their Canberra homes, but they were now meeting with a Chinese trade delegation at the Admiralty House.

39

Zhi Hui needed a cigarette after five hours of wrangling over the hundreds of details the Chinese delegation that he headed was presenting to the Australians. As he stepped out on a porch facing the harbor, he pulled a crumpled pack of Zhong Nan Hai lights from his inside coat pocket. There were two filter-tipped cigarettes left. He tapped one on his wrist to settle the tobacco then flipped open his gold-plated lighter, a present from his nephew in Hong Kong, and inhaled, filling his grateful lungs with the charcoal filtered smoke.

As he blew out through his nose and mouth, he noticed a gigantic ship moving slowly near Bradley's Head at the end of Ashley Park. He recognized the ship for what it was and thought it odd because he knew there were no LNG terminals in the harbor. He took another drag on the cigarette, pulling the ash down to his stained fingertips, stubbed it out in a sand-filled canister standing near the doors, and went back to the meeting.

40

Benjamin Taylor maneuvered his fifteen-foot Lagoon 500 leeward of Shark Island on his way back to Neutral Bay Marina after his morning sail around the harbor. He figured he could make it to the slip, change into his casual working attire, and drive across *the bridge*, and meet up with his new client in order to show her a furnished studio apartment that had just came on the market in Woolloomoolloo. The Lagoon was approaching a large ship and Taylor noticed the name on her fantail, Northwest Swan.

"Jesus," he muttered as he craned his neck to look up at the massive ship as he passed it to port.

The huge black hull towered above him, blocking out the sun and even diminishing the prevailing breeze. Taylor adjusted the sail. As he edged along the length of the ship, he noticed several bundles the size of large suitcases hanging from ropes. He wondered what they might be. Then he saw a man closely watching his progress. The man didn't look any different from the hundreds of other merchant seamen Taylor had seen on countless freighters during his mornings on the harbor over the last ten years. What was different, though, was the automatic weapon the man had slung over his shoulder. Having served as a reservist with the Royal Victoria Regiment, Taylor recognized the weapon. And being the son and brother of three lifelong merchant seamen, he knew that no crewman would be allowed to carry an automatic weapon— especially when entering a friendly port.

41

Others were beginning to notice the ship's progress through the western channel of the busy harbor. Passengers on ferries transiting across the harbor from Garden Island to the jetties around Kirribilli, watched in awe as the huge ship veered to port as it approached Robertson's Point.

Sub Lieutenant Samuel Bottoms stood on the starboard bridge wing of the guided missile frigate, HMAS Adelaide, which was preparing to get underway from its mooring in the Man-O-War anchorage near Garden Island. Scanning with binoculars across the bow of the long-range frigate HMAS Ballarat , which was moored next to the Adelaide, Bottoms noted the Northwest Swan's decks. There was something strange, but he couldn't put his finger on it. Then he noticed the harbor pilot's boat speeding alongside the ship. He could hear the faint sound of someone hailing the ship, ordering it to stop and allow the pilot aboard.

"Officer of the Deck," Bottoms called over his shoulder to the OOD inside the bridge.

The OOD stepped out on the bridge. "What is it, Bottoms?" he asked.

Bottoms pointed in the direction of the Northwest Swan. "Sir, that ship doesn't belong here."

The OOD looked where Bottoms was pointing. His lower jaw dropped in surprise. "You're most certainly correct, Bottoms." The OOD started to go back into the bridge.

"Sir," Bottoms said as he continued to study the ship.

The OOD turned back to look at Bottoms. "Yes?"

Bottoms lowered the binoculars. "There are armed men aboard and it appears there are some sorts of devices attached all along the hull. And they're wired together."

The OOD stopped, looked sharply at Bottoms. "What sort of devices?"

42

In the City of Sydney, a white van turned right off Bridge Street onto Pitt Street. The driver glanced at the rearview mirror as he passed Dalley Street on his left, and then pulled over to the curb at 30 Pitt Street in front of the Sydney Harbour Marriott Hotel. A sign on the side of the van indicated it belonged to an elevator repair company.

Kankesan Balenthiran was a recent émigré from Sri Lanka. He was also a member of the Tigers of Tamil Eelam (LTTE). He often freelanced as an assassin when not blowing up nightclubs in Bali, or other tourist attractions. Balenthiran got out on the driver's side, walked to the back of the van, and opened the double doors. He took out a large toolbox.

Moments later, he entered the hotel lobby and rode the elevator to the thirty-second floor, where he then took the stairwell to the hotel roof. He walked to the railing and with binoculars surveyed the harbor across the Overseas Passenger Terminal to Sydney Harbor Bridge.

To his right, he saw the Northwest Swan nearing Fort Denlson in the center of the harbor off Mrs. Macquaries Point. His view shifted back to the Sydney Harbor Bridge and he adjusted the focus. He could see that traffic from either direction had been halted, as he expected it would, and Special Forces were positioning themselves along the entire length.

43

On the bridge of the Northwest Swan, its captain, the lone survivor since the rest of the crew was finally killed shortly before the ship approached the harbor, stood terrified as he looked out one of the windows.

"Just keep her in the middle of the channel," Edward Bagsic ordered another guerrilla who steered the huge ship.

Police stood behind barricades at either end of Sydney Harbor Bridge. Commissioner Rhodin stood near a command vehicle listening to updates coming across his Nextel Blackberry 7520 walkie-talkie.

Stopped behind the barricades, curious drivers got out of their cars to see what was going on as Australian Special Air Service Regiment (SASR) operatives and police officers belonging to the State Protection Group (SPG), who specialized in high-risk situations, moved swiftly along the bridge, keeping below the railing so they could not be seen from the ship.

At the Man-O-War jetty, more SASR operatives jumped into four small boats and sped across the water through Farm Cove. Minutes later, they were approaching the Northwest Swan's stern.

On the ship's bridge, Edward looked out the window up at Sydney Harbor Bridge as the ship passed slowly beneath it. He saw nothing out of the ordinary. Inside the ship, a dozen heavily armed terrorists knelt on prayer rugs, while others who had finished their prayers earlier, hurried to take up defensive positions.

The swift little police boats edged up to the Northwest Swan. Operatives fired grapnel hooks that trailed ropes over the lifelines and the men were quickly aboard.

The SPG officers on Sydney Harbor Bridge watched tensely as the ship appeared to be slowing down. With traffic at a standstill and the crowds being held back, it was eerily quiet as the giant ship inched forward. Then the stillness was shattered by the sound of the ship's anchor chain clanking and scrapping as the anchor dropped away and splashed into the green water.

"Go, go, go!" one of the SPG officers shouted. Several ropes flew out and away from Sydney Bridge and dropped to the ship's main deck and superstructure. The SPG officers fast-roped down toward the ship as snipers watched from the bridge and buildings on both sides of the harbor to protect them.

Edward motioned to another man, "Get them ready. The infidels are coming and will be here soon," he said, as he pulled a Russian Makarov IZH-71 pistol from his waistband. "And take the good captain. You know what to do."

The terrorist started to open the door leading out to the starboard bridge wing.

"No, you fool," Edward hissed and motioned to the door at the back of the bridge. "Through there. Stay inside the ship."

While Edward's attention was briefly diverted, an SPG officer slid down a rope and into view right in front of the bridge window. The terrified captain's eyes widened at the sight of the hooded figure. Other SPG officers landed on the deck on either side of the bridge. The captain looked over at Edward then back at the SPG officer, who put a finger to his lips then motioned for him to duck down.

The captain knelt below the window. Edward turned just as the SPG officer fired a full burst from his M4 Assault Carbine. Edward's chest was riddled and he dropped to the floor. Simultaneously, the other SPG officers rushed into the bridge, killing two guerrillas. One SPG officer helped the captain to his feet. "Where are the explosives?" the officer said urgently.

The SASR operatives rushed forward from the fantail and immediately came under automatic weapons fire from either side of the ship. A terrorist fired a Russian RPG-7. The 85mm grenade streaked toward the SASR operatives on the starboard side. The operatives flattened themselves on the deck as the grenade exploded against one of the five LNG tanks, blasting a three-foot diameter hole.

A second terrorist started to load another grenade from behind as the shooter took aim across the ship at a second group of SASR operatives who were engaged against other terrorists. The loader slapped the shooter on the shoulder when the grenade was in place. Just as the shooter started to pull the trigger, his face exploded as a bullet hit him from behind. The loader spun around as an SPG sniper on Sydney Harbor Bridge put a bullet through his left eye.

A female terrorist—who would not have been allowed in any fundamentalist Muslim terrorist organization outside of the Philippines—knelt beside one of the bombs attached to the top of another storage tank. She looked up as one of the SASR operatives came around a corner of the superstructure. He fired at the same instant she detonated the bomb.

The operative jumped back as the explosion tore the woman in half and blew a six-foot hole in the tank. The operative had expected a massive explosion, but when nothing happened, he came back around the corner and saw the dead woman's upper torso leaning against the ruptured tank. He noticed something strange. The body was taking on a white crystalline appearance. Then he looked up at the jagged hole in the tank. The sharp metal edges were turning white, as if frozen.

"Oh, shit," he said fatalistically and reached for the mike attached to his vest. "Command, there's a breach in—"

The bullet went through his left hand and shattered the mike. A second round hit high on his protective vest, spinning him around as a third went through his neck. Then he saw a teenage boy running across the top of the tank toward him, screaming and firing his AK-47. As the operative fell to the deck dying, he managed to fire a single burst. The young terrorist's left knee shattered and he cried out in pain. He fell forward and toppled into the gaping hole. The boy's cry was cut short, as he was flash-frozen when he dropped from the balmy eight-five degrees Sydney was experiencing that day to minus three hundred thirty-eight degrees inside the tank.

44

Commuters on one of the ferries watched in fascination as the battle raged aboard the ship. Just as curious, the ferry skipper slowed the vessel in order to watch. The passengers hugged the railings. They knew something extraordinarily exciting was taking place aboard the ship that loomed over them, but they weren't quite sure just what. Then they saw the fog.

At least it looked like fog.

As a liquid, the natural gas was colorless and odorless, but when exposed to warm air it changed into a fog-like vapor that was now drifting out of the two damaged holding tanks, cascaded down the ship's side to hover above the water's surface. Then the prevailing winds pushed it away from the ship toward the surrounding cities.

Exposed to Sydney's warm air, the vapor's temperature continued to climb steadily to minus one hundred sixty-two degrees. It became less dense and invisible as it began to ascend and spread even further and faster above the surrounding cities and wharfs.

Simultaneously, the heavier, cooler vapor sank into basements, drains, and through doors into the lower floors of thousands of businesses and homes. All of this was happening in minutes, as the battle continued to rage aboard the Northwest Swan.

45

When he realized what was unfolding aboard the Northwest Swan and saw the natural gas pouring from the damaged ship, the Adelaide OOD had ordered Sub Lieutenant Bottoms to sound battle stations. The klaxon blared and the duty boatswain called general quarters over the com system throughout the ship. The crew ran to their battle stations. No one knew what was happening, but from what they could see taking place across the harbor, it wasn't good.

Bottoms heard the SH-26G (A) Super Seasprite helicopter aboard the Ballarat warming up on the afterdeck and then take off. He watched as the helo banked left sharply and headed across the harbor toward Kirribilli Point. He wondered if the prime minister or the governor-general were home.

46

Prime Minster David McGuire and Governor-General Gary Baker were standing on the lawn in front of the prime minister's residence looking out across the harbor. They had been notified that the Northwest Swan was now under siege. They did not know, yet, that two of its tanks had been breached and that Sydney was now being blanketed by an invisible cloud of potentially combustible vapor. McGuire and Baker, their staffs, and the Chinese trade delegation, could only watch as the battle unfolded before them a few hundred yards away.

Moments later, the Navy Seasprite landed on the lawn as security personnel spirited the prime minister and governor-general to the waiting helo. The head of security turned to the others. "Transportation will be here in five minutes," he shouted over the noise of the departing helo. "Be ready to evacuate. Take only what you already have with you."

As a young man, Zhi Hui had served as an infantryman in the PLA, Peoples' Liberation Army, and recognized the danger in what was happening aboard the ship. And as a senior member of the trade delegation who was directly responsible for negotiations concerning supplying his nation with natural gas, he realized that a disaster of major proportions was highly likely. He knew, as the others did not seem to know or acknowledge that they would not be able to get far enough away from the ship and its potentially deadly cargo in the next five minutes. He took out his cell phone and dialed the Hong Kong number for his nephew.

47

The Australian commandos had killed or wounded every terrorist they had found above decks and they were now pursuing more of them inside the ship. The fighting continued down each deck, as they sought out and killed the determined fanatics in the passageways and compartments. In addition to their tactical weapons, one team of four SPG officers was also armed with gamma ray dosimeters.

The man in the lead watched the LED on the dosimeter, while the others were poised for any encounter. The dosimeter gave a faint indication that they were near a source of deadly gamma rays. Each man had known going in that he was not properly protected. There had been no time to retrieve their PPE suits. Each new what little time they had left was now running out.

They turned a corner into a passageway and a man stepped out of a compartment. He had a grenade in each hand. One police officer shoved the others aside and fired, hitting the terrorist in his legs and lower torso. As the man fell to his knees, the four officers dove back into the intersecting passageway. They heard the man scream and then the grenades exploded.

The officer with the dosimeter edged around the corner and nodded for the others to follow in their original direction. The sensor began to indicate they were very close to the nuclear materials. Looking at the dosimeter, the officer motioned toward a door. "It's in there," he said as he put the sensor away and brought up his weapon. He swung the door open and they charged into the room.

Two men were hurriedly arming the bomb attached to the large pallet of encased nuclear rods. One terrorist spun around and aimed an IMI Desert Eagle .50AE at the officers. A bullet went through his heart. The other terrorist started to flip the detonation switch. He was torn apart by the deafening fusillade from all four automatic weapons. The officers rushed toward the

bomb.

48

On Sydney Bridge, Rhodin paced nervously in front of the command vehicle when a voice came over his Blackberry, "We have the ship. The device is secured."

Rhodin leaned back, rested against the command vehicle, and closed his eyes for a long moment as he caught his breath. "God was with us today, gentlemen," he said to the police officers who stood around him.

On the roof of the Marriott, Kankesan Balenthiran affectionately cradled the Barrett M82 rapid-fire .50-caliber rifle in his arms as he sat looking out toward the Northwest Swan. He hunched over and sighted in on the ship's hull through the scope. He could clearly see several figures repelling down the side as they made their way closer to the explosive charges that had been attached at thirty-foot intervals along the mid section. He focused on one of the operatives and checked the range.

The target was well within the weapon's two thousand meter kill zone.

49

Sergeant Andrew Hogen had been a member of SPG for eight years. This was the most harrowing operation he had been involved in, and all he wanted now was to get through the next few minutes alive. The certainty of this was still up in the air, but he was more hopeful than he had been during the previous hour of intense fighting.

Now that the terrorists had been killed or captured, all they had to contend with was disarming ten bundles of explosives attached to the ship's hull. His men were good at their jobs and he was confident that they would succeed. The devices weren't complicated, just dangerous if mishandled. He had six men dangling over the side and they had already deactivated four of the bombs. Hogan looked down and watched their progress as one man inched his way closer to the device directly below him.

Balenthiran snapped the ten-round magazine into place. He re-sighted the rifle on one of the explosive devices as a man drew near it. He could see another man on the deck above motioning to the one below.

Sergeant Hogan stretched, trying to relieve the tension in his lower back. In his rush to get on station when the call went out that terrorists were bringing a ship into the harbor, he had forgotten to take his twice-daily dose of ibuprofen that dulled the pain of a damaged disk. He'd have to double up tonight, he thought, as pain radiated up his back and into his groin. He looked back down at the man below.

"You about to get it, Mate?"

The younger man grinned up at him, "No sweat, Pop."

Neither man heard the shot. In the next instant, they were vaporized.

50

Rhodin and the others rushed to the railing when they heard the first explosion. "Oh, my God. What now?" he said. As they watched in horror, six more explosions followed in quick succession.

Then a voice came over his Blackberry, "We've got a sniper. He's on the Marriott."

Balenthiran eased the rifle stock from his shoulder and turned to look up as a police helicopter came in fast above him. The police sniper leaned out the door and opened fire. Balenthiran swung the rifle around, braced the stock against the roof, and fired from the hip. The .50 caliber bullet tore through the helo's Plexiglas and hit the pilot in the face, nearly ripping off his lower jaw.

The helo bucked wildly and banked sharply as it dove toward the streets below. Balenthiran set the rifle down and headed for the stairwell.

51

Thousands of Australians watched from the shoreline all around the harbor, from cruise ships docked at the Overseas Passenger Terminal, from the Opera House, and from either side of the Sydney Harbor Bridge.

Millions more watched in fascination on their televisions as the NBN-TV news helo hovered above the Northwest Swan. Few, if any, realized that they were watching millions of gallons of liquefied natural gas pouring out the side of the ruptured ship.

One mesmerized viewer who had traveled to Africa on safari the previous year thought it resembled Victoria Falls.

Aboard the frigate, Adelaide, the ship's captain, Captain Roger Elias, was now on the bridge. He lowered his binoculars. "OOD, get us the hell out of here, now."

"But, sir, shouldn't we see if there is anything we can do to assist—"

"Obey my order, Lieutenant." Elias turned to the young officer. "Do you have any comprehension of what is about to happen?" he said. "Millions of gallons of liquefied natural gas are pouring into the harbor. It is only a matter of time before it ignites. We will not be of any use to anyone if we are incinerated along with the rest of the populace. Is that plain enough?"

"Yes, sir."

Anyone who had a phone camera pulled it out and began taking pictures as the clear liquid gushed from the ship into the harbor. There was no way to warn people. A few sensed that there might be some danger to what was unfolding. Some who had experience with natural gas understood they might be in imminent peril, but even so, everyone stood transfixed as the liquid gas spread in a vast pool around the giant ship and continued to evaporate.

Balenthiran strolled through the luxurious Marriott lobby and out the front entrance. He stopped and stared at the sight of what looked like fog drifting down Pitt Street. He picked up the pace as he approached his van. As he opened the door, he noticed that the police helicopter had miraculously managed to land at a nearby park, and the sniper was trying desperately to save the wounded pilot. Balenthiran grinned, climbed in the van, and drove down Pitt Street through the fog.

52

The Australians and the Chinese delegation were getting on buses in front of Admiralty House as Zhi Hui tapped his last cigarette on his wrist and slipped it between his lips. He reached in his coat pocket and took out the lighter. As he snapped the lighter open, he was suddenly chilled. He felt clammy and thought he should get out of the breeze.

What he did not know was that the odorless and colorless vapor had already spread so rapidly and now enveloped him, the entire city, and the population as if they were a fish in a bowl. He flicked his thumb across the lighter's wheel and the spark lit the wick.

53

Zhi Hui saw delicate hues of orange, yellow, and green that warmed him in a gossamer embrace. He believed he was smiling as he wondered at how remarkably beautiful they were, in a last fraction of conscious thought, as the miniscule spark from the lighter's wheel raced outward and thoroughly obliterated him and then the entire city.

The force of the flash explosion was instantaneous. It pulsed and radiated in rolling waves like a fiery Aurora Borealis, as tongues of blinding green and orange flames flicked out thirty-five miles in every direction.

The only sound was a thunderous *whoosh*, instantly followed by a head-splitting *clap* a thousand times as powerful as the normal result of a jet aircraft breaking the sound barrier as billions of cubic feet of air was consumed and displaced.

54

Out of a population of nearly four and a half million, over seventy-five thousand died in an instant. Children on schoolyards dropped as they played. Thousands of cars and trucks collided when their drivers perished. City sidewalks were littered with corpses. Firefighters and other emergency personnel would never respond to the conflagration. Tourists died standing in line at the Opera House. Real estate agent, Benjamin Taylor, took his last breath while greeting the young woman who was eager to see the studio apartment he was going to show her. Kankesan Balenthiran watched in dismay, then horror, as flames swirled around and exploded through the white van, consuming him.

Only moments later, the secondary explosion reached deep into the very foundations of thousands of buildings throughout Sydney and every surrounding community. The heavier vapor had seeped into every crevice, crack, basement, drainage pipe, elevator shaft, and lower floor detonated. Entire city blocks collapsed and the buildings tumbled into the streets, killing thousands. Every structure along the shoreline, including the Opera House erupted as rivers of liquid fire flowed through the underground drains and vents up into the buildings.

As the vapors were consumed above and below the cities, the fires raced back to their origin—the pool of nearly ten million gallons of natural gas surrounding the Northwest Swan, where over twenty million gallons remained in its five tanks.

Even if any fire fighters had survived the initial carnage, they would not have been able to put out the fire that now swirled in a whirlpool around and the entire ship. The flames roared thunderously hundreds of feet into the sky and burned with such intensity that no known fire-fighting technique on earth would have been capable of extinguishing the inferno.

No one could stop what followed.

55

Every man on the Northwest Swan and the hundreds who had gathered on or near Sydney Harbor Bridge were already dead.

The flames continued to build and the heat increased to a point where the Northwest Swan's steel decks and superstructures began to melt and burn from stem to stern. Finally, the hull could stand no more and began to split open like a jagged festering wound along all five tanks, spilling out her cargo of twenty million gallons of liquid natural gas.

The resulting explosion registered on Richter scales worldwide. When the Northwest Swan and its entire cargo exploded, it was roughly equivalent to more than fifty of the nuclear bombs dropped on Hiroshima.

HMAS Adelaide had not escaped the firestorm as a wall of fire enveloped it and every other vessel in the harbor. The warship now drifted, a burning hulk between Hornby Lighthouse and Quarantine Head.

Every member of her dead crew was still at his battle station.

The Adelaide's Sea Sprite helo hovered above the smoke and fire that raged from horizon to horizon. Horror registered on the faces of Prime Minister McGuire and Governor-General Baker.

Sydney was gone.

56

Parris, Roy and the other surviving members of the team walked across the tarmac of the Atsugi Naval Air Facility to the C-141B Starlifter. They were joined by ten replacements that had been flown in from Okinawa at Parris's request. All were former SEALS or Marine Recon. They worked for Spartan Global Security, a private military contractor, or PMC.

PMCs provided such men to governments, small and large, around the world that either could not finance their own militaries or, as in the case of the U.S., needed people who would do what its own soldiers were not legally permitted to do.

Few Americans had heard of PMCs. In other times, in other parts of the world, they were more commonly known as mercenaries. Of course, they did not see themselves as such. They were professionals, who were hired through government purchase orders to carry out covert missions as well as act as bodyguards.

Their secretive world came under the glare of the international media spotlight on March 31, 2004, when a mob killed four Blackwater USA contractors in Fallujah, Iraq, mutilated their bodies and hung them from a bridge over the Euphrates River. Parris had known two of those men, and had worked in Iraq and Afghanistan with three of the ten Spartan contractors who joined their group now. He was glad to have them along.

As he listened on his satellite phone, the men were loading two pallets of equipment aboard the plane. He stopped and looked at Roy and spoke into the phone, "What do you mean, Sydney's gone?" He listened, stunned. Then he closed the phone and turned slowly to Roy. "There was no way to stop the fire. It's gone."

"Gone?"

"All of it."

"My god! Casualties? How many?"

"There's no way of knowing, yet."

Roy shook his head in amazement. "It will be contaminated for decades. It would appear that the theory of using an LNG ship as a weapon of mass destruction is no longer a theory. We've got to stop the others."

"We will."

The aircraft's four jet engines whined as Parris and Roy walked up the ramp. Inside, the men were securing their equipment and checking their weapons.

Later, after the aircraft had leveled off over the Pacific, Roy motioned for everyone to gather around him. He pulled a plastic-coated map out of his pack and unfolded it.

"We know that after the Hanjin Sur left Qatar, her senior engineering officer turned up missing at sea," Roy shouted above the roar of the engines and marked the ship's route on the chart with a grease pencil. "The ship pulled into Sri Lanka where Fernando Bagsic just *happened* to be in port and signed on as a replacement. Because of some curious wording in recent transmissions back to the ship's owners in Korea, they believe the ship was hijacked in the Strait of Malacca. She veered slightly from her normal course off the Spratly Islands, where they most likely took on more men." He pointed at the island of Taiwan. "They passed near Kaohsiung, zero two thirty this morning, when she suddenly changed course. The owners think she's headed for a Japanese port, possibly Osaka."

"How do they know all this, Captain?" Marchetti asked.

"The last time the Hanjin Sur was in her home port in Korea, company security techs installed a GPS system. They didn't tell the crew in order to prevent it from being disabled should it ever be hijacked. As it turned out, they were right."

"So, where do we intercept her?" Marchetti said.

Parris pointed at the chart again. "We'll link up with the others right about here, and that's where we stop her."

The men exchanged curious looks. "Others?" Marchetti said.

"Recon."

57

The Hanjin Sur's crew of fourteen was still at their stations. Each, however, was closely watched by one of the Aceh or Abu Sayyaf terrorists. Fernando Bagsic considered himself more prudent than his brothers and had decided that it would be best to keep the crew aboard as the ship made its way through Vietnam's contested waterways and then through the heavily patrolled Luzon Straight.

Now that they were nearing the Ryukyu Island chain, he was contemplating jettisoning the crew. It was now more or less a straight course to their target. He thought it highly unlikely that they would be challenged by the Japanese Navy. And since the Americans had run from Vietnam and deactivated Subic Bay Naval Station, its ships were widely dispersed throughout the Pacific.

Fernando sat in the captain's leather chair and adjusted the homemade timer. He set it for five seconds and pushed a button. A tiny red light came on and the countdown clicked from five to zero. The digital timer was hooked by wires that ran through the lid to a small battery and motor that would set in motion the triggering device attached to the daisy chain of bombs that ran throughout the ship on the outer surfaces of its storage tanks.

Satisfied with his handiwork, he closed the box and reset the timer for thirty minutes— *more than enough time to get off the ship and away*. Unlike his brothers, he did not intend to sacrifice himself. He was dedicated to the cause, but far from being a fanatic. After all, he had a young wife, and one day hoped that they might disappear in the vastness of Indonesia to raise a family. He got up from the captain's chair and slipped the timer and detonator into a knapsack.

As an engineering student, he understood more than his brothers the psychological payoff of using a *dirty bomb*. He knew, for instance, that the nuclear component of the bomb was more of a tactic deployed in order to maximize terror rather than to inflict lasting physical damage and contamination. He had even read the fact sheet the U.S. Nuclear Regulatory Commission had posted on the Internet. It stated that a dirty bomb, or a Radiological Dispersal Device (RDD), would most likely be comprised of two parts—a conventional explosive and radioactive material.

For the most part, he agreed with the statement that the conventional explosive would have more immediate lethality than the radioactive material. He also agreed that even though the radioactive levels created by most probable nuclear sources would not be high enough to kill people or cause severe illness, they would contaminate several city blocks. However, Fernando also knew that a ship transporting millions of gallons of liquefied natural gas was far removed from what most experts considered a conventional explosive device. The four pallets of spent nuclear fuel deep inside the ship were far more lethal than the typical briefcase containing pilfered radium or cesium isotopes from a hospital cancer ward or research facility.

What was even more satisfying for Fernando, though, was knowing how devastating the detonation of another nuclear device on the Japanese mainland would be for the Japanese psyche and how it would be remembered for all history. In the elite world of terrorism, Fernando Bagsic would be famous forever.

Other members of the group, both men and women, lounged around the bridge. Four men were playing a Philippine form of rummy called Cuajo. One fifteen-year-old boy terrorist was reading the latest Vince Flynn novel. He angrily ripped out a page, wadded it up, and threw it across the bridge, as he swore, "Blasphemer! I would like to meet this Mitch Rapp. I would kill him, very slowly," he shouted.

Fernando stared at the boy incredulously. "It is fiction, idiot."

"I could still defeat him," the boy glared smugly. "He defiles all Muslims."

"Do you not understand fiction? Mitch Rapp is not a real person. The author made him up. You should be angry at Flynn, not a pretend character in his books."

"Then I will kill this Flynn person."

Fernando shook his head in dismay. "You will be with Allah before the day is done. How would you carry out such a deed?"

The boy swallowed and looked at Fernando with comprehension.

"Perhaps you should spend this time reading the Qur'an, instead of this infidel's lies."

Fernando's attention was drawn to a young woman who was trying to find music on the radio when she stopped on the American Forces Radio Network broadcast from the Marine Corps Air Station, Iwakuni, Japan. A marine lance corporal was reading the morning news report of the horror of Sydney's destruction: "…an Australian spokesperson has confirmed that casualties may surpass three hundred fifty thousand deaths. Thousands more are still unaccounted for."

The terrorists broke out in wild cheering and called out, "Praise to God."

Fernando handed the knapsack to his wife, Maria, who was just finishing cleaning her M16. He walked to the door leading out to the bridge wing. Maria hung the knapsack on a hook by the door and followed him. He wrapped his arms around her and pulled her small body close to his as he stroked her hair. She closed her eyes and clung to him.

Looking out over the calm sea, Fernando thought of his brothers. He saw them as patriots, not the family of killers and fanatics that others thought of them. Since hearing the news of Sydney, he now knew Edward was dead. He could only guess what had happened to Carlos. But he knew where his youngest brother, Jessie, was, as he said a silent prayer for the boy's ultimate success.

58

Jessie Bagsic tossed the steaming glazed carrots into a saucepan. Others around him worked at preparing meals in what could have been the high-tech kitchen for an upscale New York or Beverly Hills restaurant. But the swaying of hanging pots and pans indicated that this restaurant was moving.

The head Japanese chef scurried from one end of the kitchen to the other; waiters appeared as if by magic to take the dishes of food on fine china and disappeared through swinging doors.

59

Aboard the C-141B, the men prepared two large bundles at the back of the plane. The big rear ramp opened. The men had already donned their oxygen masks, and were suiting up forward as Parris and Roy looked down from thirty-six thousand feet. At that altitude, they could see the glow of lights along the entire chain of islands that made up the Ryukyu Islands. Luckily, there was no moon. Then they saw the C-130 Hercules approaching from behind at a slightly lower altitude.

As they watched, the plane eased up beside the C-141B. They could see a man standing on its ramp, also dressed in high-altitude gear. The man saluted across the divide between them and they heard the man's voice in his headset: "Staff Sergeant Johnny Lee Walker, 1st Deep Recon Platoon, 5th Force Recon Company, III Marine Expeditionary Force reporting for duty, sir," he said with a Texas drawl. "Agent Parris, Homeland Security, and Captain Vajpayee of the Indian Marines, I presume."

Parris smiled at Roy. "Well, Staff Sergeant Walker, welcome to the party."

"Speaking of which, our briefing was...a bit brief. My boys would appreciate it, sir, if you could explain for us the nature of this mission and the rules of engagement?"

"Do you have your GPS locator with you, staff sergeant?" Roy said.

"Yes, Sir."

"Well, that little blip you see is right below us?" Parris said.

Walker noted the GPS reading, then eased out on the ramp and looked down. "Some kind of ship."

"That's right. It's a damn big ship," Parris said. "And our mission is to intercept it and rescue the crew...if they're still alive. The rules of engagement are...shoot anyone you find with a weapon."

There was a long pause, then, "Understood, Agent Parris. We'll see you below."

Moments later in the C-141B, each man checked his scuba gear, the HAPPS, high altitude precision parachute systems, and the MOLLE, modular lightweight load-carrying equipment, of the man next to him.

Weighted down with over one hundred sixty pounds of oxygen bottles, M4 carbines, .45s and 9mm pistols, ammo, communications gear, night vision goggles, medical supplies, swim fins, and other incidental equipment, they duck walked to the edge of the ramp and waited for the signal for their HALO jump.

The green jump light blinked on and each glanced at his altimeter as the two plane crews pushed the bundles over the ramp and they disappeared into the darkness. The teams leaped off the ramps into a six-mile freefall.

As they tumbled out of the C-141B, Parris glanced down and saw the marines from the Hercules plummeting earthward below him and the team.

Men and equipment plummeted at better than one hundred miles per hour toward the dark ocean. Even though they were falling, the sensation was one of floating in place and, for a few moments, Parris wondered at mankind's insignificance when compared to the brilliance from a billion stars glittering all around them and the utter lack of comprehension his species had of their precariousness on the planet below.

He forced the heavenly display from his consciousness and envisioned instead the videotaped images of the warlord, Abdul Mohammad Mohaqiq, decapitating his brother. Now he was in the right frame of mind to go back to the task at hand.

At an altitude of one thousand feet, twenty-one black stealth chutes automatically popped open. The four large bundles continued to fall a few moments more in order to be clear of the men, then their chutes deployed. As the bundles plunged into the cold water, small explosive charges cut the chute harnesses away and the bundles popped open revealing four sleek, fully loaded, fifteen-foot inflatable Zodiac CRRCs, combat rubber raiding craft.

The teams glided down toward the Zodiacs and a second before they hit the water each man pulled his quick release, disengaging from his chute, and then plunged below the surface. They swam up to the surface and over to the Zodiacs, and scrambled aboard. The marines rowed over to the others.

"Agent Parris? Captain Vajpayee?" Staff Sergeant Walker asked.

"Yes." Parris called back.

Roy gave a casual salute.

"Thanks for the invite to this little fête. Anything 5th Force Recon can do to oblige."

"Fête, Staff Sergeant?" Roy said.

Walker grinned. "Learn a new word a day, that's the goal. First time I've had a chance to put that one to use."

It was an odd scene, four Zodiacs filled with twenty-one heavily armed men intent on mayhem before the day was out, chatting. Parris checked his GPS. "I know you marines are the best at what you do, but I don't know if you've practiced for this kind of scenario, but, then again, no one has."

Of the young marines, only Walker had seen combat. "We're up to it, sir." Walker offered. "We won't let you down."

"I'm sure you won't. But you need to understand the situation." He nodded toward the horizon. "In a little over an hour, a ship over four hundred feet long and full of liquefied natural gas will be coming from that direction. We know there is a crew of fourteen. We don't know if any of them are still alive. If they are," he motioned to the Spartan contractors, "Your job is to get them off the ship and as far away from it as possible."

Parris took a manila folder out of a sealed plastic bag and handed it to Victor Brogan, one of the Spartan contractors he had worked with in Afghanistan. In his former life, Brogan was a Medal of Honor recipient, and a chief petty officer in SEAL Team Six, which was formed in 1980, to conduct counterterrorist operations at sea.

Brogan opened the folder and thumbed through fourteen photos sent from the crews' personnel files.

"Assume everyone you find is the enemy until you can compare them with those photos." Parris said.

Brogan closed the file and nodded that he understood the unspoken order.

60

A little over an hour later, the teams waited at the coordinates Parris had calculated for intercepting the Hanjin Sur. He checked his GPS receiver to make sure the ship was still headed in their direction. Then, using the night vision binoculars, he scanned toward the south. He saw the silhouette of an approaching ship, lowered the binoculars and gave hand signals to the men to get into position. The Zodiacs began to move silently at an angle to intercept the approaching ship.

Later, as the Hanjin Sur passed them, the Zodiacs sped up alongside. Fortunately, someone had carelessly left the Jacob's ladder hanging down the port side. Parris and Roy, and the marines climbed up the rope ladder to the main deck, where they were surprised again that the terrorists had obviously not felt a need to station any guards.

On the starboard side, Brogan's team threw grapnel hooks over the ship's railing. Moments later, the Spartan contractors were aboard. Brogan looked quickly in each direction for any guards. There weren't any in sight. He motioned for his men to enter the superstructure. They had been briefed during their flight so they were familiar with the ship's layout. Brogan pointed at one man, and with hand signals told him that he had fifteen minutes to find the crew and get back on the main deck by 0320.

Scotty McBride nodded and left swiftly with four of the men for the furthest door. Brogan and his team of four entered the nearest door and began working their way toward the galley. McBride's team headed to the crew's sleeping quarters.

On the other side of the ship, Parris and Roy split the men into two teams, spread out along the superstructure. They headed up three separate ladders to the second deck. Just as Roy was heading up the center ladder, a door opened and a man stepped out on the second deck. Roy froze in place, and the other men on the ladders stopped moving and breathing

Before anyone moved to take out the man above Roy, another man appeared higher up on the third deck. Roy spotted the shape of another man leaning against the bulkhead. He wouldn't have noticed the man but for the soft glow of the cigarette in his hand. Roy signaled for Singh to take the man on the third deck. Singh nodded that he understood, slipped his knife from under his clothing, and moved cat-like up the ladder to the man.

The man on the second deck walked slowly, gazing out to sea and was oblivious to the fate of his friend on the third deck as the knife flashed. Only a heartbeat separated the two men's fates. The man on the third deck didn't have a chance to make a sound as the sharp blade opened his throat. The man on the second deck coughed as if clearing his throat when the razor-tipped shaft of the arrow pierced deep into his chest.

He thought he was having a heart attack because he couldn't comprehend why he was suddenly wracked with such searing pain. He felt strange and tried to clear his head, as he started to reach out to grab the railing for support. But he was puzzled when his arms wouldn't move and hung limp at his side. *That's strange*, he thought as he looked down. It was then that he saw the black arrow sticking out of his chest. His breath caught and the arrowhead sliced deep into his heart. He toppled over the railing and disappeared into the sea.

Roy's and Parris's teams quickly linked up on the second deck. Roy was just about to lead the way up the ladder to join Singh on the third deck when another terrorist came out of the door. Before Singh could react, the man leaped back through the door and they could hear him screaming a warning to others inside the ship.

The terrorists on the bridge heard the warning, grabbed their weapons, and rushed outside. As the others disappeared into the dark, Fernando grabbed Maria's shoulder and nodded to the boy who had been reading the novel.

"Come with me," he said calmly.

61

Brogan eased around an open door leading into the crew's sleeping area. The lights were dimmed and he could hear snoring coming from the bunks. He motioned with a nod and one of his men, Terrance Sweeney, a five-foot-six former marine who grew up surfing Malibu, and held three black belts that more than made up for being height challenged, crept silently into the room.

They could hear someone in the head, turning off the shower, and then using a blow dryer. Sweeney looked around a corner and saw a man sitting in a metal chair, leaning back against the bulkhead. He had an AK-47 across his lap as he read the Qur'an, while munching on an apple.

Sweeney came up behind the man and brought up a silencer-equipped Smith & Wesson M&P 40 pistol. He looked over the man's shoulder and waited until he finished reading a page. As the man started to turn the page, Sweeney shot him behind the left ear.

Just as Brogan approached Sweeney, a woman came out of the head combing out her shoulder length, curly hair. She saw Sweeney and her dead friend, but was strangely unflustered at the site of a dead man with the right side of his face blown off. Sweeney and Brogan faced the woman with drawn weapons. She raised her hands and her towel dropped to the floor. Brogan motioned for her to move over by the bunks as another contractor began waking the sleeping men.

62

McBride and his team made their way to the galley and discovered the ship's cook, Casey Doyle, who they found out later was a former mess management specialist in the U.S. Navy. He had married a Korean exchange student and moved back to her home town of Kunsan. After a year, he had grown restless and signed on the Hanjin Sur as a cook.

When the contractors slipped into the galley, they found Doyle communing with his first love, baking cinnamon rolls. As Doyle turned, holding a full tray of hot rolls, he froze as McBride pointed a pistol and mouthed silently, "How many?"

Doyle was a cool customer, obviously relieved to see them. He grinned, nodded to his left, and whispered, "Four."

McBride led his men into the dining room where they saw three men at a table eating cinnamon roles and drinking coffee. Another man stood at a huge stainless steel coffee maker as he poured a mug full of the steaming black brew. Then they saw three more men seated at a corner table. McBride studied both groups. He didn't see any weapons.

The contractors stepped into the dinning room and trained their weapons on the men. "Everyone, stand up easy and show your hands," McBride ordered.

The three men eating the rolls stood up with their hands raised, still firmly clutching the rolls. There was a crash to his left and McBride spun around and nearly shot the man who had been pouring himself coffee. The man cringed in pain from the scalding coffee and the shattered mug lay at his feet.

McBride took a deep breath and started to ease his finger off the trigger, just as he heard an all-too-familiar sound to his right. He turned back to the three men at the corner table standing with their AK-74s.

Mark Sawaya was a competition fast draw champion and one of the deadliest shots McBride had ever seen. Sawaya shot two of the men in the corner through their hearts and would have gotten the third, but the man who had been whimpering about the hot coffee fired a 9mm Beretta, hitting Sawaya in the left temple.

Sawaya dropped, but before the terrorist could fire again, Frank Sinclair, another contractor, riddled him and the coffee maker for good measure. The last terrorist at the corner table managed to fire a single round before McBride nearly cut him in half with his Mossberg Mariner AOW sawed off shotgun. The man's mangled body sprawled across the table.

There was a clatter of pans behind them. McBride and his men turned with their weapons ready to face a new enemy only to see Doyle sprawled on the floor with his steaming cinnamon rolls scattered over him. Doyle was the single fatality among the crew.

"I don't think he'd mind if we took a couple, do you?" Sinclair cracked morbidly, motioning to the cinnamon rolls.

McBride shook his head. "You're a sick fuck, Sinclair, you know."

"I like cinnamon rolls," Sinclair protested. "They're just gonna go to waste."

"Let's get them out of here." McBride said in dismay as he motioned to the three crewmen who were still clutching their cinnamon rolls as they stood transfixed, starring at the contractors.

63

Parris' and Roy's teams were searching each compartment along a central passageway that ran the entire length of the ship. It was wider than other passageways and had rails embedded in the deck, with a single chain-fall rail attached overhead. Roy guessed that the passageway was most likely used to move heavy equipment through the ship.

As they were approaching a double door on the left, they heard someone approaching from an intersecting passageway in the opposite direction. Then they heard the sound of something sliding toward them.

The grenade careened off a bulkhead like a well-banked cue ball.

One of the marines called out, "Grenade!" There was just one problem—there was no place to go. They were caught in the open and the doors on either side of them were locked. Then Sergeant Ali stepped forward as the deadly object slid toward them. Parris only had a split second to think they were all dead, when Ali did something very unexpected. He kicked the grenade with his right toe, flung it up waist high, whirled around, and power kicked it with his left foot back down the passageway in the direction it came from.

Jaws dropped in amazement. The grenade flew through the air, bounced off the same bulkhead that only a moment before it had hit, and spun back around the corner. An explosion, followed by a flash, smoke and a screams told them all they needed to know about the fate of those who had sent the deadly little package their way.

"Goal," Ali called out jubilantly, while the others looked at him in stunned silence. He grinned triumphantly and pounded his chest with his right fist. "Forward position, East Bengal football champions. We won the Durand Cup two years in a row."

"Congratulations," Parris said.

They turned as Fernando, Maria, and the boy suddenly appeared at the opposite end of the passageway. Maria fired her M16, killing one of the marines. Ali went down, hit in both legs. Roy and Staff Sergeant Walker fired back a fusillade down the passageway. The boy was hit once in the chest and in the thigh. He stumbled back. Maria grabbed him under his left arm and the boy struggled to fire a pistol. Fernando was hit in the right hand. His thumb and index finger were blown off. Maria returned fire and the three clambered down a ladder to the next deck.

Roy looked back at Singh, "Corporal, take care of Sergeant Ali."

"Yes, sir," Singh said, as started to kneel down by his friend.

Ali waved Singh away as he looked up at Roy. "Don't worry about me, Captain," he said through clinched teeth. "You'll need Corporal Singh with you."

"I think we can spare the Corporal," Roy said

Ali shook his head. "I will be okay, sir. You don't know how many more there are."

Roy knelt down and put a hand on Ali's shoulder. "We will be back for you, Sergeant." He handed Ali a pistol.

Ali grinned through the pain and looked at his shattered legs. "I'm not going anywhere, Captain. I'll be right here waiting."

Roy patted him on the shoulder again. "Take care, Sergeant."

64

Maria helped the boy down metal stairs down to the next deck. Fernando clutched at his mangled hand. They made their way down a long passageway and stopped at a door at the end. A sign identified it as the fuel-testing compartment. Maria spun and fired around Fernando as Parris jumped across the passageway and disappeared into another doorway. Fernando shoved the door open with his shoulder and pulled her through as she kept firing at the pursuing commandos. The boy fired three times, just missing Roy. Staff Sergeant Walker fired a burst, hitting the boy again. As Fernando grabbed the boy's shirt collar and dragged him into the room, Maria fired a long burst. Walker fired high and Parris fired low as the door slammed shut.

The room was filled with high-tech fuel testing equipment and the sophisticated control systems that helped the ship run with a minimal crew. Three pallets of the spent nuclear fuel rods sat in the middle of the room. The first of many explosive devices daisy chained throughout the ship was attached to the center pallet.

Maria stood guard near the door as Fernando fought through the searing pain and looked for something to bandage his right hand. The boy was crumpled against a desk and trying not to cry, but he was terrified and badly wounded. This was not at all as he imagined it would be like to fight and die for Allah. He thought it would be quick and painless.

Maria was sorry for the boy, but she could do nothing to comfort him. She inched the door open slightly and saw a blur of movement, and fired a burst down the passageway. The doorframe around her exploded in a shower of wood splinters from return fire. A big splinter cut deep into her face. She cried out in pain as blood flowed down into her eyes, but she kept firing.

Fernando looked up at her cry. She shook her head that she was okay. He opened a metal storage cabinet and found a pile of rags and a roll of duct tape on a shelf. With a great deal of difficulty, he managed to wrap his bloody hand. The rag was quickly saturated with blood, but he was determined to carry out his mission.

He turned his attention to the explosives.

"Give me the timer and detonator," Fernando called to Maria.

She looked at him puzzled for a moment. Then she realized her mistake. She dreaded telling him, "It's in the backpack." She was crushed by the possibility that she might be responsible for their failure. She said reluctantly, "I left it on the bridge."

"You fool," Fernando swore at her.

He sat back on his haunches and shook his head in dismay. He should have kept the timer and detonator with him. Then he looked at her. She feared his displeasure more than the thought of their imminent death. He looked over at the boy, who looked back at him with a terrified expression on his fact. "Please forgive me," he said to softly to her. "It is not your fault."

"Please forgive me," she begged. "I should have thought—"

"There is nothing to forgive, my love." He smiled at her with genuine affection. "Now, you must keep the infidels away, while I attend to this," he said, motioning to the explosives.

She was grateful for his love and thoughtfulness, and turned back to the door with renewed fervor. She turned to the boy and went to his side. "Come with me." She touched the boys face and pushed his blood-matted hair out of his face. "It will be all right. We must do this together."

She helped the boy over to the shattered door and eased him down on the left side. They had a clear field of fire all the way down the passageway. "We must not let them stop Fernando," she said. "Do you understand?"

The boy clutched at his weapon and looked down the passageway, then across the open door at her. "Yes."

Maria smiled at him as a sister and turned to Fernando, who was busily searching the room.

Fernando realized regretfully that he and Maria would never disappear and raise a family as he had hoped. He believed they would not be allowed to survive even should they surrender; therefore, he saw no other recourse than to complete his jihad, and to take as many infidels with them as possible.

He looked around for anything he might be able to use to detonate the explosives and found an electrician's toolbox, opened it, and took out wire strippers, a roll of wire, and a roll of black electrician's tape. In a desk drawer, there was an unopened pack of D-cell batteries. He ripped off a piece of tape and started to wrap it around the batteries.

In the passageway, the commandos hugged the bulkhead. Roy fired a burst at the door as a marine tried to work his way down the passageway. Bullets stitched the bulkhead, barely missing the marine and he had to pull back.

"There's no cover all the way down the passageway," Parris called to Roy. "He's going to detonate the explosives if we can't take him out, real soon. They're not going anywhere. I'll keep them busy. You get everyone off the ship."

"We'll all getting out together," Roy said. He turned to the others behind him. "Sergeant Walker, take the men topside. Agent Parris and I will follow, shortly."

"You sure, Captain." Walker said. "We could lay down fire and get them out of there."

"We have no idea how close he is to detonating those explosives, Sergeant. We really don't want to be on this ship when he does."

Yes, sir," Walker said and motioned for the others to follow him out.

Roy turned back to Parris. "What do you have in mind?"

"Something rash."

"I'm counting on it, James."

As the commandos started up the ladder to the next deck, Parris took out his walkie-talkie and jammed it behind between two pipes that ran overhead the length of the passageway.

"Hey, Fernando!" he shouted. "You aren't going anywhere, so why not toss out your weapons and we'll be glad to take you into custody. If not, you'll have to live with a bad decision."

He was answered by several shots that ricocheted down the passageway.

Inside the engineering room, Fernando and Maria were surprised at the mention of his name and listened as their enemy continued to berate them, "Edward's dead and we have Carlos in custody." Fernando tore at a piece of duct tape with his teeth, then stopped working on the detonator and listened. "We couldn't shut the little fucker up. He couldn't wait to brag to us all about his three looser brothers. You can't do shit right, you know that, don't you, Fernando."

"How does he know your name?" Maria asked him.

"It does not matter," he said. He went over to the door. "You will die here with us today infidel, and my brother will strike deep into your country's heart," he taunted back. "He is like the divine wind of old that you cannot possibly stop. And what makes you think that I have failed? By Allah's will, I will succeed and bring praise on his name."

Parris shouted back down the passageway, "There's no honor in killing thousands of innocent people. You're nothing but a bunch of mass murderers. And you don't know shit about honor."

"Prepare to go to hell," Fernando's voice came back in reply.

65

Parris winked at Roy as they stood by one of the lifeboat stations. He spoke into a walkie-talkie, "If you think you're going to blow this ship in Osaka harbor, I've got some more bad news for you." The marines were helping the ship's crew into a Zodiac. Singh and Sinclair eased Ali down the side of the ship to another Zodiac. Sawaya's, Doyle's, and the marine's bodies had already been lowered to the boats.

"What makes you think I am interested in Osaka?" Fernando's voice came back over the walkie-talkie in Parris's hand. "I'll let you in on a little secret. Millions depend on the fishing fleets that come here. When I am finished, no one will be able to fish these waters for thirty years."

Parris turned as Brogan brought the girl from the shower on deck. Her hands were tied behind her back and she was still wearing only the towel. Brogan nudged her toward Parris and Roy.

"What's this?" Parris asked. "I thought we had an understanding—"

"Look at her," Brogan said. "She's not exactly dangerous." He motioned toward the towel. "And she definitely isn't armed."

The girl stood rigid between them, trying to maintain her dignity as best as she could under the circumstances.

"What's your point, Vic?" Parris said.

Brogan stepped closer to Parris and Roy. "She's only seventeen."

Roy looked at Parris, who wasn't moved by the girl's age.

"She doesn't know shit about dying," Brogan said frustrated. He grabbed the girl's arm and brought her closer. "Fine, you want her done; you do her." Brogan turned away, leaving the girl shivering in front of Parris and Roy, and headed for the Jacob's ladder with his men, as he added, "Killing stupid teenage girls ain't my style."

Parris looked at the girl and she glared defiantly back at him. The first signs of fear were beginning to replace the hatred that had been drummed into her head since she was a child.

"Was it your intension to carry out a jihad by destroying Osaka and its people?" he asked offhandedly.

She stood stiffly, trying to be brave, but her trembling lower lip gave her away as she declared by rote, "It is the duty of all Muslims to destroy the infidels."

"Whatever." Parris shrugged. He turned away from her and spoke into the walkie-talkie, "Kiss the little lady good-bye, Fernando. It's time for you to go to hell." He looked at Roy, "Let's go." He motioned for the others to leave. Parris took a satellite radio out of his vest and pushed a button to speak, "Seawolf, this is Echo One, do you read? Over."

A moment later a reply came back, "Echo One, this is Seawolf, Roger, we copy. Over."

66

Fernando turned from working frantically on the triggering device when he heard Parris' voice echo down the passageway again, "Fernando, you ever hear of the Ryukyu Trench?" He looked at Maria, wondering what the American was getting at. "I thought you would like to know that we are right over the Ryukyu Trench, which is twenty-four thousand six hundred feet straight down." Fernando turned back to the triggering device. Maria came over and stood beside him. He looked up at her. "In case you can't figure that out, that's over four miles, right under where you're standing," droned on.

67

The others were in the Zodiacs. Only Parris, Roy, McBride, and the girl remained on the deck of the Hanjin Sur. The girl's composure had dissipated along with her bravado. Her face was wet with tears and she was trembling.

Roy took the girl's chin and raised it so he could look into her eyes. She reminded him of his daughter, who was two years younger. "Is it still your desire to die for Allah, at this time?"

She tried to hold firm to her beliefs, but it just wasn't in her. She shook her head, no. Roy looked at Parris, who let out a sigh, rolled his eyes. "Let's get out of here." He glanced at the girl. "Her, too."

Roy smiled and turned to McBride. "She has apparently had a change of heart, Mr. McBride. Will you please escort her off the ship?"

"You got it." He took the girl by the arm. "Let's go, sweet cakes."

"This is the only second chance you'll get." Parris said as McBride led her to the side of the ship. She stopped and turned to Parris and Roy.

"Thank you."

"You should think seriously about this the rest of your life, young lady," Roy advised.

A few moments later, Parris and Roy stepped off the Jacob's ladder into the waiting Zodiac. As it sped away, Parris switched the frequency on a radio. "Seawolf, she's all yours."

The voice of the submarine's commanding officer answered, "Roger, Echo One."

68

The first of her kind, the USS Seawolf (SSN-21), with a crew of one hundred sixteen, hovered one hundred feet below the surface and two thousand yards from the Hanjin Sur. With twice as many torpedo tubes and carrying thirty percent more weapons than a Los Angeles-class fast attack submarine, the Seawolf was designed specifically to kill Soviet ballistic missile submarines. With the fall of the Soviet Union, she was relegated to patrolling the waters off North Korea and China, should the day come that she might be needed to take on the growing naval power of these two belligerent countries.

Captain John Brenner, the Seawolf's commanding offer called out the order, "Fire one,"

"Fire one," came the response from the torpedo room over a speaker, closely followed by three more commands and responses.

A spread of four Mark 48 Mod 7 ADCAP wire-guided torpedoes raced toward the Hanjin Sur. What made these particular torpedoes different from their predecessors was not only a concern for the ecology, but also the U.S. Navy's discovery of reverse engineering.

69

Over the past decade, the U.S. Navy had secretly managed to retrieve the remains of three Russian submarines. The subs had sunk because their underpaid and poorly trained crews had run them into seamounts or they had been blown apart from their own runaway torpedoes. Because the Russians were incapable of recovering their subs due to a lack of expertise of deep diving submersibles, the Navy had concluded that there was a treasure trove to be had from retrieving these sunken technological secrets.

The concept had its beginnings in 1968, after a Soviet Golf-class ballistic missile submarine mysteriously sank one hundred fifty miles northwest of Hawaii in seventeen thousand feet of water.

Using a cover story of mining for deep-sea nodules of manganese, Howard Hughes cooperated with the CIA to push forward what was called the Deep Ocean Mining Project. At a cost of over two hundred million dollars, the platform ship, Glomar Explorer, was built in 1973. On June 20, 1974, the Glomar Explorer found the Soviet submarine and an attempt was made to bring it to the surface.

Of course, the Soviets knew exactly what the Americans were doing, but not wanting to broadcast to the world that they had lost the sub in the first place, they were content to monitor the operation as it progressed.

To say the least, the Russians weren't disappointed when an accident caused the weakened hull to break apart as it was being brought up and it sank, taking its most of the nuclear missiles and the crypto codes with her back to the bottom. The CIA did manage to recover several missiles and torpedoes, along with the sub's code machine.

After the media discovered and broadcast to the world the Glomar Explorer's *failed* attempt, the Navy went deep, literally, as it became more adept at finding and retrieving sunken subs without being detected by the Russians—or the media.

During this time, it also became more apparent that there might be, on occasion, times when happenstance or inept seamanship was not enough, and U.S. intelligence forces would be required to use the direct approach—sink them.

Capturing a submarine or other warship on the surface was out of the question. The political fallout would be messy and there was always the risk a determined crew might decide to fight back. Sinking a ship, though, had its advantages, particularly if it could be made to look like an accident or force of nature.

A clever government weapons technician came up with the bright idea of the *ball-buster* torpedo, as it was nicknamed. It was designed to strike a vessel near the keel. The resulting blast from the acoustic, shape-charged torpedo would be directed downward. The explosive material within the torpedo was a new compound that delivered an ultra-frequency sonic punch. The futuristic technology transformed the ship's steel hull to a brittle, glass-like material, that would easily shatter, which resulted in the ship sinking in record time.

70

Unaware of what the Americans had in store for them, but realizing it would be very unpleasant, Fernando had finished working on the triggering device. He was attaching it to the explosives and continued even as his tormentor's voice chided, "Fernando, do you hear that noise?"

Fernando stopped and listened. At first, he couldn't make it out. Then he did hear something—a distant whining sound. He looked over at Maria. Then Parris' voice gave him the bad news, "That is the sound of four very special torpedoes headed your way. You can kiss your girlfriend good-bye."

71

Each of the nineteen-foot, three thousand four-hundred-fifty pound torpedoes raced at over fifty knots toward the ship's hull. Each trailed thin wires behind that continually guided them from inside the Seawolf.

They struck the hull simultaneously thirty feet below the waterline. Instead of exploding on impact, though, their diamond-hardened casings pierced the ship's double hull and continued to gouge their way deep into the Hanjin Sur as they crashed through bulkheads, compartments, and machinery, opening up the ship to the sea.

Water rushed in through the thirty-foot tear in the side of the ship and began to fill the compartments as the torpedoes came to rest amidships, fifteen feet above the ship's keel. The water was part of the design as it played an important role in helping to dampen any fire that may result when the torpedoes finally detonated.

From the commandos' vantage point in the Zodiacs, two hundred yards away, when the explosion came it wasn't all that impressive and they looked at one another curiously. Roy shrugged at Parris.

"That was certainly anticlimactic," he wondered aloud.

Then they heard the ship begin to groan—deep inside.

72

The force of the explosion threw Fernando and Maria to the deck. He looked at the triggering device and the wires dangling and realized he had failed.

"Let's go," he said, thinking the better part of valor was to survive the day in order to strike again at another time, another place. They rushed out of the engineering compartment and ran down the passageway.

The commandos continued to watch the Hanjin Sur. Nothing seemed to be happening.

"Is that all there is?" McBride said. "I was hoping for..." he searched for the right phrase and could only come up with, "more of a bang."

Parris looked at his watch, then at the men. "The show has only just begun."

Beneath the ship, the hull's metal skin started to give way and the bottom of the ship cracked like a pane of glass and fell away.

Fernando and Maria were thrown violently against a bulkhead as the deck started to tilt sharply upward. Maria screamed. They slid uncontrollably down the passageway and crashed into a bulkhead.

The commandos, the ship's crew, and the lone girl watched as the ship floundered, tipped over on its starboard side, and began to slip beneath the surface.

"Now, that is impressive. How did they manage to accomplish that?" Roy wondered aloud.

Parris smiled slightly as the ship continued to disappear beneath the surface.

"It's a secret."

"You crafty Americans. Always coming up with ingenious ways to break things and kill people."

"It's a gift."

Maria clung desperately to Fernando, terrified by the sound of water rushing through the ship toward them.

"God is with us," Fernando whispered, already accepting their fate. He pulled his wife closer to him and buried her face in his chest as he watched down the passageway in anticipation.

Then a wall of water careened around the far end of the passageway and rushed at them. As it advanced, lights exploded.

The last light went out and they were plunged into darkness.

Maria screamed.

73

A week later, at the Department of Homeland Security, Eric Stone, John Langella, Parris, and Roy were gathered in Command Information Center. Stone brought an image up on a flat screen. The face was that of the youngest of the Bagsic brother, Jessie.

Stone turned from looking at the boy's smiling image on the screen to the group. "His name is Jessie Bagsic. He's the youngest of the four brothers, but from what we've been able to discover, he's also the most radical. He was the first to join Abu Sayyaf. He then recruited his brothers and his father to join."

"He's been attempting to establish closer ties with Al-Qa'ida," Langella added. "I think we can conclude after Sydney, that he was successful."

"Only through your team's efforts," Stone said to Parris and Roy, "in sinking the Hanjin Sur, was Japan spared the same fate as Australia."

"I'm sure the ship's owners weren't all that thrilled about losing their ship," Parris said.

"They have already submitted their claim to Lloyds," Langella said. "It was a small sacrifice from the Japanese' perspective."

"Does anyone know what will happen when the ship begins to break up a few years from now?" Roy asked.

"The gas will rise to the surface, but from the best we understand it, the environmental affects will be negligible," Langella said.

"How can that be? Thirty million gallons of natural gas..."

"At that depth, even if there should be a spontaneous release of the entire load, it will be sufficiently diluted and won't be much more than a burp compared to methane that is released naturally."

"A burp?" Roy looked at Parris.

"That's a technical term," Parris quipped.

"Yes, I thought so." Roy smiled.

"Let's not pat ourselves on the back just yet," Stone said. "We still have to run the last brother to ground. Do we have any idea where he's headed or his intended target?"

"They seem to favor these LNG ships," Roy said. "Could we not simply track down each to see if he has infiltrated the crew?"

Stone took a folder out of his desk drawer and handed it to Roy. "Last count, there are over one hundred sixty LNG ships spread around the world," he said as Roy studied the list of ships and their owners. "Some, but not all, of the owners have clamped down on security since nine-eleven. Lord Burkenshire has set up a real-time reporting system."

Langella pushed a button on a desk-mounted control panel and eighty-seven LNG ships that had a GPS system installed appeared on the screen as red dots, with their name beside them. "These are the ships that have the GPS security system." He studied the map for a second. "And, as of this very moment, there are no incident reports."

"What about the ships that don't have GPS?" Parris asked.

Langella punched another button. Longitude and latitude readings appeared on the map.

"Lord Burkenshire's people monitor course settings that are now being reported hourly, since Sydney. It's not exactly real-time, but it's close enough. So far, we have no incident reports."

"Can you highlight those ships in U.S. waters?" Parris' eyes narrowed as he studied the map.

Langella pushed a few buttons and almost all of the ships disappeared, leaving just three in the Gulf Coast near Texas. Another one was moving along the East Coast off Virginia, and a fifth was approaching Hawaii.

"There's no terminal in Hawaii," Roy said. "Why would an LNG ship be going there?"

They studied the display. "She's the Zephyrus," Langella said as he brought up the ship's information on the computer screen. "She's headed for the new LNG terminal that just went online at Long Beach to Hawaii."

"What did you say the name of the ship is?" Stone asked.

Roy put a finger on the image representing the ship heading. "The Zephyrus."

Stood thought a long moment. "Either of you two read any Greek mythology?"

"But of course," Roy said.

"Yeah, high school stuff. You know, the Iliad and the Odyssey," Parris said.

"You wrote in your report that Fernando referred to Jessie as a 'divine wind.'" Stone touched the name of the ship on the computer.

Roy's eyes showed recognition. "Of course, Zephyrus, the West wind. But you do not have to go all the way back to ancient Greece." He thought a moment, then quoted from one of his school boy lessons, "When April with his showers sweet with fruit the drought of March has pierced unto the root, and bathed each vein with liquor that has power, to generate therein and sire the flower; when Zephyrus also has, with his sweet breath—"

Parris turned to Roy and continued the famous piece, "quickened again, in every holt and heath, the tender shoots and buds, and the young sun into the bull one half his course has run, and many little birds make melody that sleep through all the night with open eye so nature pricks them on to ramp and rage—"

"A Wyoming cowboy who quotes from Chaucer's *Canterbury Tales Prologue*?" Roy said. "I might have imagined you would be more at ease with Edward O'Reilly's *Saga of Pecos Bill*."

"Mom was a high school lit teacher, and a poet in her own right." Parris studied Roy. "You've actually read the Saga of Pecos Bill?"

"If you two are quite finished with the literary corner," Stone interjected. "Chaucer aside, in the Greek myth, Zephyrus competed against Apollo for the love of a Spartan prince. When the prince chose Apollo instead, Zephyrus was mad with jealousy. One day the prince was throwing a discus and Zephyrus blew a gust of wind that caused the discus to strike the prince in the head, killing him."

"Zephyrus was known as the gentle, benevolent force, in contrast to his violent brother, Boreas, the North wind," Roy said.

"Until he became enraged, then Zephyrus killed," Parris said. "A divine wind that kills. Sound familiar?"

"Yes, quite," Roy agreed.

"Jessie is on the Zephyrus," Parris said. He turned to the others. "And it's anchored just outside Pearl Harbor." Then he looked at the wall calendar. The others followed and saw the date.

"December 7th!" The significance of the date stunned Langella. "The entire Pacific Fleet is in port. Hundreds of thousands of tourists and veterans are there."

"This can't happen," Stone said. "Not again."

Parris stood to leave. "Not if we can help it." He motioned to Roy. "You still in the game, my friend?"

"In for a penny, in for a pound." Roy said as he stood.

"We've got a long plane ride."

"How can we be sure that we will arrive in time to stop him?" Roy looked at Stone. "Perhaps we should notify local authorities—"

"You boys get suited up and I'll get your ride." Stone said as he reached for his phone.

"He will most likely carry out the attack when he can do the most harm and the world will see it live on TV," Parris said.

"You two get over to Langley ASAP. You'll have time to spare." Stone said cryptically.

Parris and Roy exchange a curious look. Stone waved them to move. "Go."

As Parris opened the door to leave, Stone was saying to someone on the other end of the line, "Harry, I need you to fire up Aurora."

Roy glanced back at Stone at the mention of Aurora.

74

Parris and Roy stood in the cavernous hanger, transfixed at the massive black aircraft. A hydraulic-powered trap door opened under the aircraft and the pilot stepped out. Wearing a high-altitude pressure flight suit, he stood five feet six (the better to fit in tight cockpits). In his mid fifties, his hair was long and red. He didn't look like a typical Air Force pilot. He wasn't. Harry Saxon's life was as secret as the aircraft he tested and flew during covert operations.

Saxon held out a hand to both men. They shook hands. "I hear you fellows need a lift."

Parris motioned toward the aircraft. "What is that thing? I've never seen anything like it."

"I believe it is the Aurora." Roy answered eagerly. Roy was obviously enraptured at being in presence of the ultra-secret aircraft. He turned to Parris. "You do not realize what this is?"

"Well, it sure isn't the Concorde. But since it looks like an offspring of the SR-71 Blackbird and the F/A-22 Raptor Stealth Fighter," Parris said. "I'll take a wild guess and say it's the latest spy plane out of Area 51."

Roy ran his hand along the sleek aircraft's fuselage, almost affectionately. He looked at Saxon. "It is the Aurora, isn't it?"

"You've heard of her," Saxon said proudly.

"Oh, yes." Roy looked into one of the huge jet engines. "She is much, much more. Is it true that she can exceed an altitude of more than two hundred thousand?" He looked at Saxon for confirmation.

"Oh, she'll get up in that neighborhood, I suppose." Saxon said coyly.

"Some neighborhood," Parris said with awe.

"She is a long-range reconnaissance follow-on to the SR-71," Roy recited from memory. "She has a blended delta wing with seventy-five degree leading-edge sweep and retractable low-speed fore-planes. It is thought that she is most likely powered by two regenerative air-turbo ramjet engines."

"I'm impressed," Parris said.

"You've been surfing the Net," Saxon said. "Don't believe everything the conspiracy blogs have to say."

Roy wasn't put off by the remark. It only encouraged him. He looked up the hatch into the aircraft. "Is it true she will do Mach six?"

"Mach six?" Parris said as he tried to calculate the numbers. "That's, what, a couple thousand miles per hour?"

"Over four thousand miles per hour," Roy said almost gleefully.

"Give or take, depending on the altitude and air temperature," Saxon said.

"That's fast." Parris smiled.

A test pilot of long standing with the CIA, Saxon was justifiably proud of his newest toy. "Give her a good tailwind at thirty-seven miles up and she's the fastest commute on the planet," He said, then asked, "How long did it take you to drive over here from down town?"

"A little over an hour," Roy said.

"Less than an hour ago, I took off from Groom Lake, on the West Coast." He touched the side of one of the engines with the back of his right hand. "She's still warm."

Roy and Parris exchanged an appreciative look.

"You boys up for the ride of your lives," Saxon said.

"I wouldn't miss it for the world," Roy said.

Saxon pointed to a locker room. "You'll find your flight suits there. We take off in twenty minutes."

"We need to be at Pearl Harbor ASAP," Parris said.

"No problem. But this baby only flies at night or at extreme altitudes," he said. "I'll have to drop you boys off on the fly, if you know what I mean."

75

They were still climbing nearly straight up and had left the stratosphere behind. The Aurora leveled off twenty miles into the mesosphere. It was minus ninety-nine degrees outside the aircraft, but inside the men were comfortable in their heated pressure suits. In twenty minutes they were already somewhere above Iowa, following the curvature of the earth.

Roy felt like he was personally involved in his own conspiratorial wet dream, as he looked down at the million points of light across the United States, and the scattered lights of the comparatively underdeveloped Canadian wilderness.

They watched in awe as hundreds of meteors burned up as they collided with the billions of gas particles that were found in the mesosphere.

As they drifted on the edge of space, Parris glanced out the right side of the cockpit and saw what looked like thin, wispy clouds. They glowed electric blue. "What's that?" he asked.

Saxon's voice came over his headset, "Noctilucent clouds. Some called the night shining clouds."

"They're beautiful," Roy said.

"They're the highest clouds in Earth's atmosphere," Saxon said. "Scientist don't know that much about them."

"I'd think it would be a little hard to get up here to study them," Parris said.

"Right you are," Saxon came back. "This is pretty rarified air space. Me, and a select few from NASA, are the only ones who get a chance to come out here and play."

Saxon tilted the aircraft slightly so they could get a better view of the phenomena as he continued his travelogue, "Some think they're made up of volcanic or meteoric dust. Scientists noticed them around 1885, after Krakatoa blew its top. Now some think it might be water exhaust from the Space Shuttle."

"You're kidding," Parris said.

"That's what I've been told." Saxon checked his gauges. "Time for a pit stop. We could make it just fine to the islands, but after I drop you boys off, I'm due over the land of Mullahs, so I need to top her off."

Saxon eased the controls forward and the Aurora began a slow descent. By the time they rendezvoused with the Air Force KC-767 Tanker, they were over Idaho.

Floodlights blinked on the engine and on the wing pylons. The refueling boom began to snake out behind the tanker. Saxon eased the Aurora up until the two aircraft were coupled, like mating birds.

"Top her off, please," Saxon radioed to an airman monitoring the refueling from inside the tanker. "High test, if you please."

"Check under the hood today, sir?" the Airman said.

"No need. I take care of the oil and tires myself."

"Roger that."

"Much obliged. Can you do the windshield while you're at it?"

"We're not that full service, sir."

At six hundred gallons a minute, the Aurora was topped off in ten minutes.

"There you go, sir. Have a safe flight," the Airman said as the boom disengaged and pulled back into the tanker. "Navigator says it's clear sailing all the way."

The Aurora dropped back from the tanker. Saxon pulled back on the controls, and once again, they were headed up.

"Next stop, the big island." Saxon said.

"Real chatty up here," Parris said. "Who'd of known?"

"You'd be surprised who you run into up here," Saxon said. "It gets real crowded, sometimes."

"I bet."

"If you guys are into power naps, now would be a good time. We're racing the sun."

"Who could sleep," Roy said.

"Not me," Parris said. "It's not every day I get to fly with super spook in his testosterone-powered space plane."

The Aurora pulled up out of the darkness that cloaked the Earth and began its race against the rising sun.

76

Saxon eased the Aurora down to thirty thousand feet and slipped into the clouds.

"Watch that first step," he said. "It can be a killer."

Parris and Roy disconnected from the plane's oxygen supply and connected to the bottles strapped to their chests, pulled their parachute harnesses tight, and crossed their arms over their chests. "Let's do it," Parris said.

77

Sunrise services had taken place two hours earlier at the Pearl Harbor Memorial Chapel, Submarine Memorial Chapel Pearl Harbor, and Naval Chapel Barbers Point. Buildings and street signs were decked out in red, white, and blue bunting in preparation for the December 7th memorial festivities.

Bunting also hung from the ships and submarines that were in port. Moored along the piers of the submarine base where the Bremerton (SSN 698), Cheyenne (SSN 773), Honolulu (SSN 718), Los Angeles (SSN 688), and Tucson (SSN 770). The Port Royal CG 73 was just pulling into Pearl Harbor. Moored in pairs west of Pearl Harbor Naval Base were the cruiser, Chosen, (CG 65), destroyers Chaffee, (DD 90) and Hopper (DDG 70), frigates Commelin (FFG 37) and Rueben Parris (FFG 57). Tied up to the Naval Base piers where the aircraft carriers Abraham Lincoln (CVN 72) and Ronald Reagan (CVN 76).

Two battleships were forever at their stations along Ford Island. USS Arizona (BB 39), with many of her crew of eleven hundred seventy-seven still aboard, rested in a state on the bottom as flags were set up and an honor guard rehearsed inside the memorial above her. A thousand yards from the Arizona Memorial, aboard USS Missouri (BB 63), a museum volunteer polished the Japanese surrender plaque embedded in the teak wood deck.

Across from the Naval Base, tour buses crossed over Admiral Clary Bridge to unload tourists on four hundred fifty-acre Ford Island at the center of Pearl Harbor. Along the airfield tarmac, mechanics sipped on steaming cups of freshly brewed Starbucks and prepared to put the finishing touches on five Boeing F/A-18 Hornet aircraft for the Blue Angels demonstration team.

And for the first time, two Japanese warships, the anti-submarine destroyer, DDK Yamagumo, and the guided missile destroyer, DDG Hatakaze, had been invited to take part.

While there were protests at the Japanese presence, few of the old veterans and survivors of the attack objected when the two warships tied up to the Naval Base piers.

Fabulous yachts and sailboats were anchored throughout the harbor as party boats for the rich and famous. One yacht, the Magic II, flying the blue, red, and white flag of the Kanto Yacht Club, was covered with the beautiful people from Hollywood, New York, and Japan. At over one hundred twenty-two feet long, and having been recently purchased for thirteen million dollars from an Australian entrepreneur, she was the most luxurious party platform in the harbor.

Celebrities and celebrity wannabes were already sipping champagne, lounging in bikinis, and enjoying the sumptuous breakfast. Their host, Izumi Mifune, a Japanese action movie star who adopted the last name of his idol, the late Toshiro Mifune, made the rounds.

The fact that he was an action star was obvious because of a huge cutout poster depicting Mifune with full-body, pseudo-tattoos that occupied a corner of the main deck. He was promoting his latest film. Not unlike other films he had made, it was causing controversy back home because some critics claimed it glamorized the Yakuza gangsters. It had long been rumored that, not unlike Sinatra and the American Mafia, Mifune was associated with the Japanese gang in some way.

Though he often frequented the Ginza nightclubs, which were controlled by the Yakuza, Izumi Mifune was not "officially" connected. He had garnered the attention of the Sixth Yamaguchi-gumi, the supreme Godfather of Japan's largest and most powerful Yakuza. The man admired Mifune much the same way that some of the American Mafia had appreciated Marlon Brando's portrayal of Don Vito Corleone in *The Godfather*. Apparently, though, the Sumiyoshi-ikka, an affiliate organization, did not hold Mifune in such high esteem. Its leader had managed to see a sneak preview of the film and he was not pleased.

78

Aboard the aircraft carrier, USS Ronald Reagan, chairs were being arranged on the flight deck in front of a grandstand where a country band was warming up for the afternoon's performance.

At the same time, at twenty-five thousand feet over Pearl Harbor, Parris and Roy were plummeting through the three-thousand foot thick cirrostratus clouds. Even with high altitude pressure suits, goggles, and the facemasks protecting them from the elements and supplying them with oxygen, it was bone-chilling cold. They were flying blind because their entire bodies were covered in a layer of ice crystals, so they could not appreciate the brilliant halo that encircled the sun as it showed through the nearly transparent clouds.

Ensign Perry Kipler scanned the sky overhead with his binoculars. He had received the call only two hour ago that he was to get his men from SEAL Team Three ready to link up with two spooks who would be *dropping in*.

His men were already aboard three Little Bird helos, warmed up, suited up, and ready to go. Kipler was wondering how "real" the operation was. SEALs were constantly practicing for their next mission, and he only knew that the spooks would have the details for what he was told was to be the highest classified operation he had ever been involved in.

He was also wondering why they were making their entrance in such a potentially public way and on a day when there were sure to be thousands of cameras that might capture their involvement. He didn't like it, but he wasn't given a vote.

Then he saw them. They were just two black specks as they emerged from the clouds—still freefalling. He wondered how ballsy the two were. How low would they get before popping their chutes? He continued to follow the two as they fell earthward.

Their goggles were clear now and they could see Pearl Harbor Naval Base, Ford Island, and Hickam Air Force Base. Parris glanced at his altimeter. They were at fifteen thousand feet as they dropped with their arms at their sides to increase their speed and direction. Parris glanced over at Roy.

"There it is," he said in his radio, meaning Ford Island. Roy nodded that he understood.

Suddenly, they heard the roar of a powerful piston engine and their view of the harbor below was blotted out as they stared down into the cockpit of a Mitsubishi A6M Zero.

Parris jerked to his right and could see the pilot's blue eyes bulge behind the goggles in surprise as he streaked by the aircraft. Roy barely cleared the plane's tail and the pilot twisted in his seat trying to see what had just dropped out of the sky and almost collided with him.

Parris rolled over so he was falling backwards and saw that Roy had safely cleared the Zero. Then he watched in amazement as Roy came within inches of being squashed like an insect on the canopy of a dull green Curtis P-40 Warhawk. The nose of the fighter was emblazoned with painted sharks teeth and it streaked behind the Zero firing its twin .30 caliber machine guns.

"Holy shit," was all Ensign Kipler could say as he witnessed the near miss.

On the Battleship Missouri, a tourist from Kansas City had been videotaping the approach of the two World War II aircraft as they rehearsed for the dogfight that would take place over the harbor later in the day. He saw what he thought were two skydivers who barely missed being killed by the two planes. He kept taping, already thinking about where he was going to sell the footage should they be killed. Part of him was praying for the skydivers to survive, while another part was thrilled at the prospect of seeing his video on the evening news.

The SEALS in the Little Birds watched intently as the two figures continued to fall.

"Any time would be good," one said aloud what all were thinking.

"They don't do it soon, they're going to be buried head first up to their assholes," another SEAL said.

At one thousand feet, Roy's chute deployed. Parris veered slightly to the left to place himself closer to the Little Birds. He pulled his release at eight hundred feet. His chute barely opened and as his feet hit the ground. He hit the quick release, and walked toward Ensign Kipler as the chute settled to the ground.

Roy landed to Parris's right a couple seconds later.

Inside, Kipler was very impressed. Outwardly, he remained stoic as he motioned toward the Little Birds. Parris and Roy headed for one of the helos. Parris handed out black and white photos to men getting into the other helos, and then jumped aboard the third and hooked up to the communication system so he could brief the SEALs as they flew out to the ship.

"I won't go into the 'this is a matter of national security' routine. You all know we wouldn't be going through this little exercise unless it was. The photo is of the guy we want. His name is Jessie Bagsic. He's a member of Abu Sayyaf and he intends to do some serious damage here today."

Inside a gleaming, stainless steel galley, Jessie scooped sherbet into small desert dishes.

Parris continued his brief, "We have good intel that he is working aboard the Methane Princess, which is carrying liquefied natural gas."

"Is this ship like the one that blew up in Sydney?" one of the SEALs asked.

"Yes, it is." Parris looked at the faces of the men in the helo with him and Roy.

"And if he has his way," Roy added, "he will achieve the same results as his brother did in Sydney."

"That's why we're here," Parris said. "We're going to stop him."

Another SEAL asked, "Where is this ship right now?"

"She's in Mamala Bay anchorage, just outside of Pearl. He signed on as a cook just before the ship left Singapore."

Jessie emptied the container of sherbet and tossed it into the trash. He walked through the galley to a door with stairs that led down to a cold storage compartment.

"We're pretty sure that he has a nuclear device and plans on detonating it during the Pearl Harbor celebration." Parris said. The three Little Birds skimmed the harbor.

79

Jessie stepped into the huge freezer and threaded his way through stacked crates of frozen vegetables, shrimp, and fish. He set down his backpack, and set aside several cases of frozen foods, revealing two large wooden boxes stenciled Tajima-ushi Kobe Beef.

At more than a thousand dollars a pound, each box was easily worth over six hundred thousand. He took a meat hook and lifted several slabs, uncovering the metal case. Then he checked the wiring to the C-4 charges, pushed two bare ends through a small hole in the wooden box that he had drilled earlier, and took the timer from his backpack. He set the timer on a box of frozen pees so he could see the digital readout. Then he pushed a button. A tiny red light flickered on and the countdown began at thirty minutes.

Unlike the missions of his brothers, Edward and Fernando, Jessie's mission was not to bring utter destruction to Pearl Harbor. Only those in the immediate vicinity of the yacht would be killed outright. But to contaminate a major U.S. port city and vital military installations that were home to nuclear missile and fast attack submarines, as well as the entire 7th Fleet for decades would be a major blow against the infidels.

As he turned to pick up one of the boxes, he had set on the floor, his feet went out from under him and he fell hard against a wooden box, knocking the wind out of him and cutting his left hand on a jagged edge of a pallet. He took a few breaths to calm down, got to his feet, and noticed his bloody palm.

He started for the door and slipped again. This time, he was able to keep from falling. He studied the floor and saw a thin sheen of ice covered by frost. On closer examination, he saw that the ice was a result from a water leak coming from under the wooden pallet on which the boxes were stacked. He studied the ceiling and saw two heavily insulated pipes that ran the length of the freezer. One of the pipes had a small leak and a long icicle hung down below it. A drop of water fell and disappeared behind the stack of boxes.

He looked at the timer. Fifty-seven seconds had passed.

He looked again at his palm and decided he needed to bandage it. He left the freezer and as the door clicked shut behind him, the light went out.

The only light in the room now came from the red numbers as they kept clicking off the seconds. The low drone of the refrigerant compressor filled the freezer.

There was another sound, though. The drip, drip, drip of the leaky pipe.

80

"We believe that he may be planning to detonate the device to coincide with the time of the December 7th attack," Roy said as the Little Birds cleared the island and headed out to sea. "That gives us only," He checked his watch, "thirty-five minutes. We do not think there are any other Abu Sayyaf members onboard the ship, but we cannot be sure. We have to take him alive, at all cost. It is a big ship and he is the only one who will know where the device is located."

Aboard the vessel, Jessie stepped into the galley with a fresh tub of sherbet and dropped it onto the stainless steel countertop where he continued filling the desert dishes.

"He is a fanatic of the first magnitude." Parris looked at the SEALs' faces. They were all young and eager. Failure was not an option. "Any questions?"

"What about evacuating?" one man asked.

"Not possible," Kipler said. "Half of the 7th Fleet is in port and thousands of veterans and their families are here, not to mention the fact that there are hundreds of boats scattered throughout the harbor."

"Anyone else?" Parris asked. No one spoke up. There was no need. They all understood what lay ahead of them. "Good. Let's roll."

The Little Birds swooped passed several cargo ships anchored in Mamala Bay. The SEALs sat in open doorways with their feet braced against the skids; their weapons at the ready.

81

Jessie finished scooping the sherbet. Waiters took them and headed out of the galley. He cleaned his work area. When finished, he took his apron and the tall paper chef's hat off and left the galley. He could hear music and laughter coming down a staircase, glanced up the ladder, and saw a woman's legs under a short skirt.

Celebrities and other partygoers aboard the Magic II watched as a Bell 430 helicopter lifted off the yacht's landing pad on its way to Honolulu Airport to pick up a Hollywood producer and his entourage.

In the freezer, the timer continued to count down: 25:45.

82

The Methane Princess was anchored two miles from the coast. On the main deck, technicians tended to the myriad of pipes, valves, and gauges, while seamen busily cleaned and painted the ship's outer surfaces in the never-ending battle against the sea salt that caused rust and corrosion.

Jessie opened his personal locker in the crew's berthing area. He hung up his apron and threw the paper hat into a trashcan. He took out a Walther PPK pistol, shoulder holster, and a Micro Uzi. He reached up on the shelf, grabbed a six-inch boning knife and a cleaver, and slipped them into his belt.

"What are you doing down here?" a voice demanded. Jessie spun around and smiled at the Japanese head chef as the man approached him. "You're supposed to be in the—."

The chef stopped in mid sentence when he saw the Uzi in Jessie's left hand. What he did not see was the boning knife in his right hand. Jessie struck swiftly and the chef staggered back as his intestines spilled out onto the floor. The chef tried desperately to hold them, thinking the effort might somehow save him, as he fell to his knees, then toppled over on his side.

Jessie looked down with uncaring eyes at the gasping man as his breathing slowed, then stopped. He turned back to his locker and removed two green, jar-shaped MK3A2 grenades, putting them in the side pockets of his baggy cargo pants.

Then he dragged the chef's body into a storage space and stuffed it in with the mops and cleaning gear. He went back to his locker where he took out a prayer rug, closed the door, and then snapped the padlock shut. He spread the rug on the floor, knelt down, and began his last prayer.

83

The Methane Princess's engineers and seamen were startled as the black Little Bird helos seemed to rise from the sea and appeared on either side of the ship. Ropes dropped from each and in five seconds, Parris, Roy, and the entire SEAL team had fast-roped to the main deck. They screamed at the ship's crew to get down on their bellies. The frightened men hugged the deck as the commandos straddled them and checked their faces against Jessie's photo.

The timer in the freezer read: 21:20

Jessie folded his prayer rug and placed it on his bunk. He used a pillowcase to wipe the chef's blood from the boning knife.

The Methane Princess' crew was still sprawled on the deck as each was checked against the photo. After the last man was examined, Kipler called out, "He's not here."

"Who are you looking for?" the ship's captain challenged.

The commandos turned to see Roy leading the captain down from the bridge to the main deck. Parris stepped up to the captain and held up the photo. "This man signed on as a cook."

The captain glanced at the photo only a second. "He's no longer a part of my crew."

"What do you mean?" Parris challenged.

"He signed on in Singapore," Roy said.

"Yes, he did. He is an excellent cook. I hated to lose him, but he said he got a better offer. He left the ship during our layover in Guam."

"Guam?" Roy said.

"That doesn't make any sense," Parris said. He turned to Roy. "Why would he stay in Guam?"

"I did not say he stayed on Guam," the captain said.

"But you said he got a better offer in Guam." Roy said.

The captain shook his head. "No, he did not get an offer in Guam. He boarded another vessel in there."

"Which one?" Parris asked.

84

Jessie approached the stairs leading up to the music and laughter. He appeared at the top of the stairs and found himself in the middle of a throng of well-healed socialites, celebrities, and hangers-on, all caught up in the party atmosphere.

No one took any notice of him. He walked strode among them like an unseen lion about to pounce on its prey. A waiter did not recognize him and offered him champagne. He declined and glanced at the huge cardboard three-dimensional display of the Mifune in his roll as an undercover cop who infiltrates the Yakuza.

Jessie thought how surprised the action star was going to be when he learned that the Yakuza had decided Mifune must pay the ultimate price for the insult. Then he tapped a finger on the shoulder of a statuesque blond. She turned from talking with a handsome American leading man type and smiled at Jessie. Then she looked at him curiously, as if to ask 'who are you and why are you bothering me?'

She screamed as Jessie suddenly grabbed her lustrous hair, yanked it hard, exposing her long, graceful neck, and slit her throat. Blood spurted out, spraying several people. A woman screamed. Heads turned to see what was going on.

Jessie took out his Uzi.

Aboard the aircraft carrier Ronald Reagan, the country band was in full swing, playing a very rousing, and very loud, song. The audience was totally enthralled by the performance. So much so, that no one noticed people jumping from and falling from the Magic II.

Another party was taking place on a somewhat smaller yacht a few hundred feet from the Magic II. Everyone turned at the sound of shooting and screaming. They leaned against the railing and saw someone shooting at people on the Japanese actor's yacht. Bodies were falling into the harbor. Those who managed to escape by jumping were swimming for their lives as they screamed for help.

Aboard the Magic II, the deck was covered with the dead and those who would soon die. Jessie aimed the Uzi at Mifune, who was traumatized by the slaughter surrounding him. The actor knelt next to the body of a young Japanese woman. Then he looked up at Jessie and fury replaced his torment. He stood slowly and faced the killer.

"Murderer!" he shouted in English. "Coward!" He clinched his fists and started toward Jessie, who raised his weapon and smiled at the actor.

"This is not one of your movies," Jessie said. "And you are not the good guy."

Mifune's rage overcame his fear as he continued to move toward Jessie. For the first time in his life, he was not acting. He was prepared to fight to the death, which seemed imminent.

Jessie aimed the Uzi at Mifune's chest. He started to squeeze the trigger. Then his left shoulder exploded from a heavy-caliber bullet.

Jessie spun around, tripped over the body of the blond who was the first of the Hollywood crowd to die, and crashed into the bar. He couldn't understand what had just happened to him, as agonizing pain shot through his shoulder. He felt like his body was on fire as he looked toward the back of the yacht and saw a black helicopter hovering. A man was aiming a rifle at him. Jessie struggled to get to his feet and raise the Uzi.

Parris fired again.

Jessie left leg was blown out from under him. He fell and squeezed the Uzi's trigger, tearing up the teak wood deck until the clip emptied.

Mifune staggered and fell to the deck, as the commandos fast-roped down to the yacht. They quickly disengaged from the ropes and as they started toward the carnage, Jessie staggered toward them with a grenade in his right hand. Blood ran down his arm and over the grenade. He pulled the safety clip and his left index finger curled through the pull ring.

"You cannot stop the will of Allah!"

A primal scream erupted behind him, startling Jessie for an instant. He turned involuntarily and was amazed to see the wounded Japanese actor flying through the air at him. Mifune spun and kicked Jessie in the face.

Knocked off balance, Jessie stumbled to the side. Not to be defeated, he yanked the pull ring, arming the grenade.

Parris and Roy fired at the same instant.

Jessie's body jumped in the air from the impacts, but he still managed to flip the grenade at them before collapsing to the deck.

The grenade toppled end-over-end through the air at them. The SEALs, who were closer to the railings, reacted instantly, leaping over the side. Parris and Roy were caught standing flatfooted and ankle-deep in the carnage. They knew they would never make it and that they could only watch as the grenade tumbled toward them.

85

Then Roy shoved Parris aside and dove for the grenade. He caught it in mid air, hit the deck, rolled, and came up on one knee. He threw the grenade underhanded in the opposite direction the SEALs had jumped, out over the water, where it exploded harmlessly.

Parris stared. Stunned. Roy stood up and looked at him, grinning broadly. "Soccer is okay, but I prefer cricket. Though, that was not one of my better tosses."

Parris didn't realize that for the last few seconds he was holding his breath. "Good enough for government work, my friend," Parris said, taking in a deep breath.

They turned at the sound of Jessie moaning. Parris knelt down and pulled Jessie up roughly. Jessie smiled through the death veil, as blood oozed from his mouth and pumped out of his chest with each beat of his dying heart.

"Where's the bomb?" Parris demanded.

Jessie's face filled with peace. "You are too late." He choked on his own blood.

Parris shook. "Tell me, you sonofabitch, where is it!"

Jessie's eyes fluttered and started to close. Parris shook him again and his eyes opened slowly. A little smile came across his lips.

"The freezer." He started to chuckle, but it was more of a gurgle. "You cannot stop it. It is Allah's will..."

Then he died.

Parris and Roy turned to Mifune.

"Where's the freezer?" Roy said.

"Down the stairs, in the galley, then down another deck."

They ran to the stairs and leaped down to the next deck, then sprinted down the passageway. They ran across the galley and jumped down another set of stairs. At the end of the short passageway, they saw the freezer. It was a foot race to the stainless steel doors.

They slid to a stop in front of the freezer. A massive padlock hung from the handle. Parris yanked his Glock and shot the lock away, grabbed the handle and swung the door open. Fog rolled out into the passageway.

They stepped inside.

Crates of frozen vegetables and other goods were stacked along the walls. Pork carcasses hung from hooks. They shoved the meat aside, fanned the fog with their hands, and looked in every direction. As they tossed boxes aside, Roy saw the red digital timer counting down: 00:15…00:14…00:13…00:12.

"There it is." He could barely control his voice as his mind raced along with the numbers counting down.

Parris shoved the box that covered the metal box aside and he saw the entire device was encased in ice. He glanced up and saw the pipe dripping water down a long icicle. He looked around in desperation.

"What?" Roy said. He couldn't take his eyes off the digital countdown.

"Ice pick, hammer, anything!"

Both looked quickly around the freezer. Nothing.

Parris yanked his pistol from its holster, flipped it so he could hold it by the barrel and hammered at the ice with the handle. Ice chips flew in every direction, but it was not enough.

The timer continued: 00:005…00:04…00:03.

Parris knew he was helpless to stop it. He stood up and looked at Roy in resignation. They both watched the time.

CLICK!

They had run out of time and stared a long moment at the glowing red numerals: 00:00

Both jumped back involuntarily as three explosions went off and the yacht vibrated. For an instant, they thought they must be dead. Then they realized they were still standing there and what they were hearing were the underwater explosions coming from the reenactment of the Japanese attack and realized that the Japanese Zero must have had dropped the dummy torpedo moments before. The underwater detonations were meant to simulate a torpedo explosion.

They looked back at the timer.

It still read 00:00. The clock had stopped

Then they knew what had happened. Parris knelt down by the device and raised the gun to strike it again.

Roy's hand reached out and stopped Parris' hand in mid swing. Parris looked up at Roy, who was firmly holding on to his wrist.

"You don't really want to do that," he whispered, fearful that even his voice might reactivate the device. "Do you?"

At the sound of something cracking, Parris looked up just as the thick icicle broke off and fell, shattering on the floor. They glanced at the thermometer that hung on the wall near the open door. What little remained of the fog hugged the floor. The temperature inside the freezer was rising.

They leaped for the door. Both grabbed the long handle and yanked the door shut. As it snapped shut, the overhead light went out and they were in total darkness.

As their eyes adjusted to the darkness, they began to detect a faint red glow a few feet away. The red digital numbers that meant the difference between life and oblivion remained frozen on 00:00.

They could hear fireworks. Both men sighed in relief.

"We're missing the show," Roy said.

"I've had enough fireworks for one day," Parris answered.

86

Fireworks exploded over Ford Island behind USS Ronald Reagan. The country band played a rousing version of the Star Spangled Banner, as American Idol winner and Nashville star, Carrie Underwood, belted out the last words of the anthem.

Hundreds of people stood on the immense flight deck and cheered as the Blue Angels demonstration team blasted overhead in their gleaming five blue and gold F/A 18 Hornets, separated, spun on their axes, and flew straight up into the blue sky.

Behind the carrier, the SEALs helped Mifune into a Little Bird on the yacht's flight deck. As Parris and Roy watched, the helo flew away. A second Little Bird landed and the remaining SEALs boarded and left.

The third Little Bird came in, and hovered a few inches above the flight deck, as Roy and Parris stepped onto the helo's skid, and it lifted off.

Epilogue

Karim Abdullah Yousaf was an educated man. He was also a Shia Muslim. When the Taliban came looking for him, he fled the country and went to Pakistan. Eventually, he immigrated to the United States. After the Taliban had been defeated, he felt compelled to return to help his country recover from the years of blood letting and tyranny.

In his wildest dreams he would never have imagined he might one day end up working as the secretary for a man he considered a defiler and murderer. But these were still desperate times for the Islamic Republic of Afghanistan, and the Karzai presidency was being threatened by a Taliban resurgence be mounted in the northern Faryab province.

So, alliances of convenience had been formed to bolster up the government. One such alliance was with the former warlord, Abdul Mohammad Mohaqiq, the defiler, as Yousaf thought of him with disgust.

Yousaf sat behind his desk and tried to keep from hearing the girl's crying and pleading. He was ashamed and he could not look at the woman seated nearby who had procured the girl for Mohaqiq.

He busied himself with paperwork for Mohaqiq, who had replaced a recently assassinated cabinet member. Yousaf suspected that Mohaqiq was behind the murder, as did the Kabul police chief, who recruited Yousaf. As one of Kabul's newest police officers, he prayed five times a day that Mohaqiq or one of his followers would not discover he was working undercover.

While attempting to build a case for the assassination, Yousaf quickly discovered that he was powerless to do anything about the debauchery and brutality that was taking place in Mohaqiq's residence on a daily basis.

Mohaqiq's depravity and sexual appetite for children was beyond Yousaf's comprehension. Each night, after he left the residence, he would report to the police chief what he had witnessed or heard.

The chief said he understood Yousaf's concern, but he was determined to prosecute the former warlord for assassinating the cabinet member. The chief did not tell Yousaf that the cabinet member was his cousin.

Yousaf turned as the huge double doors leading to Mohaqiq's quarters opened. The woman stood as the girl was ushered out. *She couldn't be thirteen years old*, Yousaf thought and prayed to himself that he would not go to hell for his part in the betrayal of the child. He thought of his inability to protect her from this monster as a betrayal to his people and to his faith.

Mohaqiq motioned for the woman to approach. The girl cringed beside him. He took her roughly by the shoulder and pushed her toward the woman.

"This one is *too* experienced," he said. The woman understood his meaning—at thirteen, the girl was too old.

"I have a new one just this morning," she said business-like. "She is unspoiled and quite beautiful. For an Uzbek. I will bring her to you this evening."

"Have her here after Isha'a," he said, concerning the evening prayer.

"As you will," she said as she guided the traumatized girl from the room.

Mohaqiq looked at Yousaf and rubbed his ample belly.

"I am hungry," he said and went back into his quarters as Yousaf picked up the phone and pushed the button to the kitchen.

Mohaqiq thought that he must find another source. Obviously, the woman did not have sufficient contacts to procure the young girls he must have. But he could not risk using local girls. Besides, he preferred village girls who were more likely to cooperate and keep silent because their widowed mothers had sold them into prostitution in order to feed the children still at home.

He wondered what was keeping the cook. The girl had protested and begged him to allow her to leave, but he had satisfied himself and now he was famished. He looked around the room and thought of how far he had come from his days as a minor warlord. He was prepared to use any means to assure his place in the cabinet. And perhaps one day he would seek the presidency. *Anything was possible.*

He was admiring his form in a full-length gold mirror as he adjusted his tie. He would have to talk to his tailor about the fit of his new suit. Then he thought he saw a movement in the mirror. His glasses were on his desk and he squinted. He saw a glimpse of the jeweled sword he had brought with him from the north.

A dark figure, wearing a black hood, appeared behind him. Who dared enter his residence, he thought.

Then he saw the eyes.

He remembered those strange colored eyes. He shuddered. *Impossible.*

He started to turn and the light from the desk lamp reflected off the long, curved blade of the sword. Mohaqiq was suddenly dizzy. The room began to spin out of control. He could not understand what was happening. *Why did he feel so strange?*

Then the room began to bounce wildly. He was spinning out of control on the floor.

I must have fallen, he thought as the spinning sensation began to slow down. It was difficult for him to focus and he had a strange sensation that his body was floating.

Then he saw the body in front of him. There was something familiar about it. Then he realized that it had on a suit just like the one he was wearing. And the same tie?

He tried to scream when he saw that the body had no head. But his severed vocal cords would not permit him to scream.

As his eyes began to cloud, the man stepped out of the shadows, removed his hood, and Mohaqiq saw the blond hair—and those eyes.

Parris dropped Mohaqiq's bloody sword near the severed head and he left by the window.

Made in the USA
Charleston, SC
09 February 2012